Mining Mill Murders

Shelia Bryson

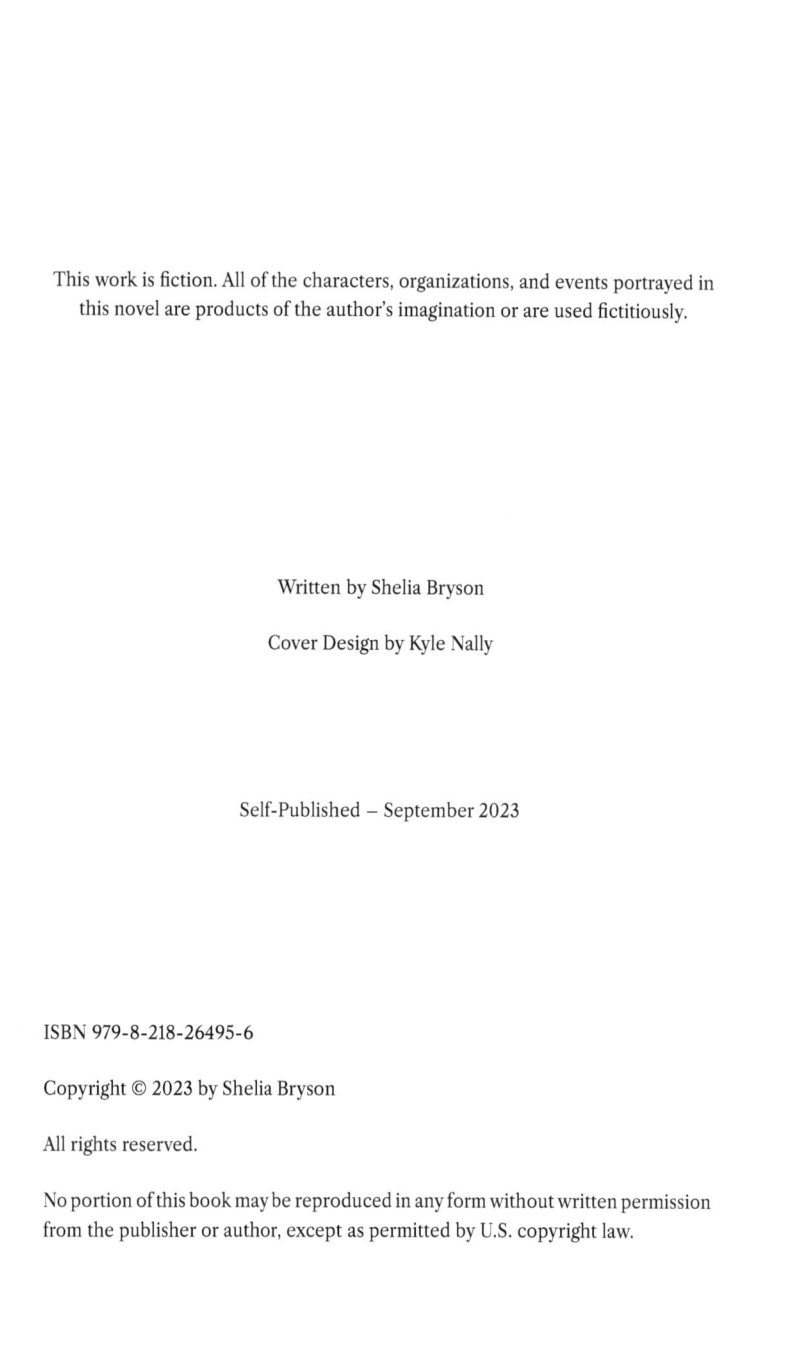

This work is fiction. All of the characters, organizations, and events portrayed in this novel are products of the author's imagination or are used fictitiously.

Written by Shelia Bryson

Cover Design by Kyle Nally

Self-Published – September 2023

ISBN 979-8-218-26495-6

Copyright © 2023 by Shelia Bryson

All rights reserved.

No portion of this book may be reproduced in any form without written permission from the publisher or author, except as permitted by U.S. copyright law.

This book is dedicated to my children. Harley, Dora, & Trey
I love you guys and y'all mean the world to me.

Also, I dedicate this book to my sweet daddy, who is no longer here with us. You will be forever missed.

Finally, my wonderful grandbabies. Omie loves y'all so much!

Greetings from the Author

I want to thank you for reading my book. I enjoyed writing it and I fell in love with each of my characters. This is my first book, and I can't wait to hopefully write more. When I started my writing journey, it was unexpected. I want to personally thank all the folks that helped me make my dream a reality. My family and friends' encouragement were the push I needed to complete this. To all of them, I thank you for listening to my million conversations about this story. A special thanks to those that read my story and provided me with feedback. The list of my loved ones and friends is long. I couldn't have done it without their help. I hope you enjoy the story as much as I have enjoyed writing it.

Shelia

A special thanks to my friends and family. You all played a generous role in my book, and I will forever be grateful.

Jackie McCullar (Thank you for believing in me and all of your help and hard work!)

No matter how the world views my success, I am successful because I am surrounded by so much love.

Kyle Nally

Harley Parker - Clay Nally

Susan Wood - Stacy McCain

Brittany Brown - Angie Ellison

Dylan Winship - Steve McCullar

Tommy Adams - Gretchen Adams

Margaret Stanley - Trey Moore

Chapter 1

IN A SMALL SOUTHERN town, nothing ever changes. Here, time seems to stand still. Tonight seemed different though. Something was off.

It was January and a cold front was moving into the area bringing below-freezing temperatures and the threat of snow and ice. Everyone would be panicking and racing to the stores for groceries and gas with worries of being stuck at home for days. Although this may seem like extreme behavior to many, Georgia just isn't set up to handle hard winter weather conditions.

Here, winter weather rarely happens. Everyone fears they may get trapped in their homes until the roads are cleared. Most of the backroads would not even be plowed and they would be impossible to travel. Often, it also meant the power would go out as trees would fall on the power lines.

Brooke should be at the grocery store tonight as well. Instead, she was headed to Mining Mill Park.

The park was a recreational center used in this part of the county. It was always busy with activities for the community, from basketball games to baseball games and more. Since so much was always going on at the center, it usually meant no one would notice who was or wasn't there.

For Brooke, it meant no one would notice her or the man she was meeting. It was a meeting that filled her with anxiety and excitement all at the same time.

She parked in the back area of the lot, where several cars were parked. She wanted to blend in. As she looked in her review mirror, she applied one last little touch-up of lip gloss and one more spritz of perfume. She was blushing at the thought of what she was doing.

Brooke was not familiar with the situation she was in. Sneaking around made her uncomfortable, and she hated lying to the people she loved and mostly hated what her son would think of her. She readied herself, unbuckled, and headed to the black SUV waiting behind her.

"Hey, you." Tom greeted her with a smile.

"Hey." Her voice was weak and filled with nerves, but she smiled back as she climbed into his vehicle.

Brooke had run into Tom at the November Push Sales Conference. They spent their entire time at the conference together. His first words had surprised her, as he had told her she had taken his breath away. He had called her beautiful.

They had met several times over the past month and a half. Both of them found comfort in their meetings. They would hold each other and compare life stories. It was wrong, but neither of them could fight the feelings they were experiencing.

Tom reminded Brooke of her youth and a simpler time in her life, and now she felt young again. They had grown up together and attended the same schools. After graduation, their adult lives took them in different directions. They both ended up settling down back here in Willowville, but had only seen each other in passing. They hadn't spoken since she left for college.

Being with Tom also reminded Brooke of her dad. Growing up, their families shared many times together. Brooke's dad had been her world. When he passed away, the whole community mourned. Now, even all these years since his passing, Brooke's heart was still broken, and she ached to have one more hug from her daddy.

They drove out to an old road off from the park, a road she hadn't thought of in so many years prior to these meetings with Tom. When they were teens, they used to sneak out here all the time, often to drink.

Tonight, they stayed longer than normal. They laughed as they chatted about their younger years, times at school, old mutual friends, and the teenage parties they had both attended.

"Do you remember the night that we partied at Shirley's house?" Tom grinned as he asked. "Her parents had gone out of town, and you girls had about twenty people over at her house."

He assumed she had forgotten - it had been so long ago. Shirley was her best friend, and they were always together.

Brooke blushed as she thought about that night. "Yes, of course, I remember. That was my first real kiss. I'm surprised that you remember that night."

"I didn't know that I was your first kiss. But I do know that I never forgot that night or that kiss. I remember we snuck down to the barn and talked for hours," he paused. "I also remember you seemed a little reserved around me after that night."

"Oh, Tom. I was just too nervous and thought it didn't mean anything to you because I was so young. That was the summer before I started high school. I couldn't have asked for a sweeter first kiss." Brooke smiled, thinking that kiss had been more special than she realized at the time.

"Brooke, I always thought you were beautiful from the time we were in elementary school. I always found ways when we were growing up to go to your house with my dad."

They both agreed that the night at Shirley's house was a night that still held a special place in both of their hearts all these years. Their chemistry had been electrifying that night.

Like the last several encounters, they spent time talking about the past and the present. They both shared things that had brought them to this point. They spoke of their personal lives, families, children, and even marriages. Brooke and Tom both confessed they felt terrible, but they were both so caught up in the moment, the guilt seemed small in comparison to the other feelings they were experiencing.

"I wish I wasn't battling this guilty feeling, because being with you has been amazing." Tom admitted.

"I feel the same way." Brooke agreed.

Tom pulled Brooke close to him. As always, the seats in his SUV kept them from holding each other as close as they would like.

Tonight, he needed her to be closer. "We could sit in the back." Tom nervously suggested as he looked at Brooke's long legs. "But if you don't want to, I understand." Tom paused as he watched her face.

Surprisingly, Brooke nodded yes but didn't dare say a word. She didn't trust herself to speak, afraid she would say no.

They got out, and Tom put the back seats down to give them more room. As they held each other, their lips met for the first time since that high school kiss. Tom pulled her in and stroked her long hair. He kissed her ear, trailing those kisses down her neck. Brooke moaned. Their passion erupted as they began stripping and caressing each other. Their bodies joined and they made love.

Afterward, as they looked into each other's eyes, they now wondered what their futures would hold.

"I am so sorry that our times together have only been in my car. I wish things were different." Tom apologized. "You deserve better than this."

Brooke giggled with excitement as she responded to him. She was still giddy from the experience she had just had, and her body was still tingling. "That was mind-blowingly crazy and wonderful. I feel alive for the first time in so many years." She still couldn't believe how intense it had been.

When they pulled back up to her car, later than they both intended, the lot had cleared more than normal. Most people had hurried home before the roads iced over. Brooke hugged Tom one more time, trying to suck in as much of him as she could, not knowing when she would be able to meet him again.

As she started out of the car, she looked over at Tom and smiled at him.

"Thank you, Tom." She whispered to him.

"Be careful going home, Brooke. I will text you as soon as I can."

They both knew that could mean days because they had to be careful when they were around their families.

Being her goofy and clumsy self, Brooke dropped her purse as she was getting out of his SUV. She laughed as she gathered her stuff as fast as possible from the ground before anyone saw her. Then with quick laughs from both again and one last kiss goodbye, she headed to her car with her keys in hand.

Tom watched her all the way to her car. She was strong and independent, but she looked at life with childlike eyes. She was truly gorgeous inside and out. Brooke had a natural beauty. She was six feet tall with long black hair that hung down her back. He remembered that even when they were young, people noticed her when she entered a room.

Once Brooke was in her car, her laughter turned to tears. Watching Tom drive off, her mind was racing. All the thoughts of guilt, shame, and yet a joy that she hadn't felt in such a long time. A feeling of being listened to and the feeling of being wanted. Brooke had not been intimate in many years with her husband.

The bedroom had not been a pleasant place in her home. Joe was rough and never cared about her needs. He had complained to the point that she thought something was wrong with her body. She now knew that nothing was wrong with her. Her face warmed as she thought of Tom.

Sitting there, she realized it was much later than planned. She started pulling through the now very empty lot. She knew that she needed to check in at home. At that point, Brooke realized her phone was missing. She started to panic but thought it must have dropped out when her purse had fallen.

She u-turned her car and returned to the area where Tom had been parked. She drove around and thankfully spotted it. It took her a minute to get her vehicle lined up to grab it without getting out of the car. She thanked God she hadn't run over it when she had backed out.

As she reached down to put her car back in drive, she noticed in her rearview mirror, a man standing there looking at her. Between the drizzle and her nerves, it seemed impossible for her to make out his face. However, she was sure he wore an orange toboggan and seemed tall. It was hard not to notice the bright orange.

She did not know how long he had been standing there watching her. She panicked at being seen and possibly being recognized. She quickly put the car in drive and punched it out of the parking lot.

She tried to focus on the roads as they were getting slick. Her mind was racing now. Her husband, Joe, was going to be raising hell at her. Where were the groceries, and what had she been doing for almost four hours? Brooke knew that Joe didn't usually need a reason to be raising hell! He was angry at her all the time.

Her mind turned to the man she had seen in her rearview mirror at the park. Why had he been standing behind her car, and what had he seen? It made no sense for anyone to be in an almost empty parking lot with the sleet and rain falling like it was.

She blushed again, thinking about the passion she had shared with Tom. She had never had that response to lovemaking before. Although, she had nothing to compare it to, as she had only been with Joe.

Brooke looked down and realized her gas light was on. She had forgotten to get gas on her way to the park.

"Son of a biscuit!" She cursed out loud.

She was irresponsible when it came to getting gas. There had been so many times that she had almost run out. Thank God, it had only happened once.

That time, she had been on her way back home with Frankie, her 12-year-old son, from the doctor's office. They had run out about two miles from her driveway because they lived so far away from a gas station. She had called a towing company, and they had charged her sixty dollars for two gallons of gas. She swore then she would be more responsible. And yet here she was turning back around to go fill up.

After she filled her tank, she got back on the road home. Her car was almost sliding off the road from the ice. She called her son's phone, but he didn't answer. She assumed he was probably too busy playing video games with his friends to worry about answering her. By the time she was pulling down her long driveway, she thanked God that she hadn't wrecked.

Walking into the house, or more like sneaking in, seemed to take part of the joy out of seeing Tom.

Luckily, the living room was empty when she came through the front door. Her son, Frankie, was sound asleep in his bed with a gaming controller in hand as she peeked into his room. She stood watching his breathing. He was the most important part of her life, and he kept her going during times when she wanted to quit. Adulting with a sick parent, and a hard marriage, took a lot of energy.

She didn't go into her bedroom, but from the hallway, she could see that Joe lay passed out on top of the covers with his clothes still on. One benefit of his over-drinking meant he would sleep all night long. He was an alcoholic, but no one knew that, and he would never admit it.

Locking up for the night, she noticed the sleet had turned to snow. It was already sticking. Snow was always a beautiful sight when you rarely saw it. The snow glistened and sparkled as the light in the front yard glared down, reflecting on it. She wished she wasn't so worked up so that she could just go sit on her porch. The porch was her favorite spot of the house. But now, she was too drained from overthinking everything.

As Brooke sat down on the couch, with her mind still on the last several hours, she knew her choices of late would affect Frankie. She never wanted any pain to come to him and prided herself on being his mom.

If it was just Joe and not Frankie, she wouldn't care because Joe deserved bad things to happen to him. Joe was a snake, and you never knew when he would strike. He was not just an alcoholic - over the years, she slowly realized he was also a narcissist. Really, if she didn't need the money for her mother's care, she would have gotten herself and Frankie away from Joe a long time ago.

Still on the couch, she soon fell asleep. She awakened to a grown man grumbling, a TV blaring, and an overly excited boy yelling at the top of his lungs.

Before she could even get herself into an upright position, her son dropped beside her on the couch, almost landing on her. His voice shouting, "Nothing ever happens like that here!"

She stretched into him for a hug as she asked, "What are you yelling about, honey?" How he had grown so much lately, she beamed with love at him.

"MOM, three people were killed last night! It's on every TV station. They were shot at Mining Mill Park."

Brooke almost fainted.

Chapter 2

BROOKE TRIED TO FOCUS on the TV as the reporter spoke.

"Reporting Live from Willowville, this is Brittany Brown."

Brooke thought the reporter was a beautiful lady, but looked a bit out of place standing at the corner gas station next to the park.

"Last night, two men and a woman were found dead at Mining Mill Park. The police are not giving out any information at this time, but according to a local county employee who found the woman, she appeared to have suffered a gunshot wound to her head. He also heard another officer say the other two bodies had the same gunshot marking."

Eric Stinson looked stunned, standing behind the reporter. He was too shaken up to even speak since he was interviewed.

Brooke had known Eric since she was little, even though he had been several grades ahead of her. She smiled at the memories of Eric buying her and Shirley alcohol when they were seniors in high school.

Eric had always had a thing for Shirley, and Brooke was sure that Eric would have done almost anything they asked back then. She felt horrible for him. He must be so confused and scared, finding a dead body. No one could ever imagine something like this happening here in this town.

Looking down at her phone, locals were already blowing up the internet with posts. Some claimed it was a serial killer. This was why she tried to stay off of social media, no one knew any facts yet, but here they all were with their opinions.

Brooke put the phone down. All this news made her feel sick to her stomach. Was there a serial killer on the loose? Frankie was right – this kind of stuff didn't happen here.

Apparently, the only information the police had released so far was that the woman had been found close to the gym building, and the men's bodies were laying towards the wood-line area. Again, her thoughts went to the park and meeting with Tom, then to the man in her rearview mirror.

Suddenly, Joe jolted her back into focus.

"Good thing that someone didn't come in shooting up the grocery store last night. You would have been shot because you talk too much. Dumbass redneck woman was shot because she wouldn't shut up! Live at 11!"

His evil laughter filled the room.

She snapped at his laughter. "Joe! What a nasty thing to say now in this moment! How could you joke about this? People are dead, and here you are trying to make me feel stupid. What is wrong with you?" Brooke was almost yelling.

Luckily, Frankie was in the kitchen and hadn't heard his father's comment. It was so hard to keep Frankie away from all this negativity.

She looked over at Joe, now stretched out in his recliner. He was handsome, but the alcohol had aged him. He had always been very clean-cut. He was also very athletic looking, although Brooke didn't know if he worked out or not. She rarely knew where he spent his days, whether he was at his law firm office or down in his garage. It was best to avoid conversations with him. If she asked the wrong thing, it would start a fuss. Nowadays, she just tried to keep to herself and stay busy with Frankie. She didn't like having to constantly defend herself to Joe.

He was what she called "a street angel and a house devil." Despite what she knew about him, people loved Joe. He had a charm that he laid on thick in public. In the beginning, Brooke had fallen for Joe's appeal as well.

They had met at her friend's party at the university she attended. Brooke was showered with Joe's attention initially, always making her feel like he cared. They had a few very ugly arguments that she made excuses for, but the good seemed to outweigh the bad.

Joe was an attorney at his family's law firm in the metropolitan area. He had finished law school faster than anyone she ever knew. She had been so proud of him but never understood how quickly he had gotten a law degree. Joe was smart, but Brooke always assumed his family's money and connections had helped make that happen.

Joe came from money. He liked to brag and thought he was better than everyone else. He was born and raised in the metro area. Growing up in the big city, he had lived a different life than she had. She had been raised to be modest, kind, and grateful for everything she had. Her family had never done without, but didn't have the extravagant things Joe was accustomed to. Country life was simpler, and Brooke loved it that way.

Joe always let her know he was the smart one. He had even nicknamed her his hillbilly when they were dating. A name he would still reference when he was being mean. Why had she thought that was once cute? She now knew it was never meant to be endearing. He wanted to make her feel less than.

Early on, he would make her call him to let him know she had made it safely to her destination. If she accidentally forgot, he would cuss her out, and then use the excuse it was because he loved her so much and worried about her safety.

He was always turning the blame on her, but now she saw the truth. He used it controllingly because he wanted to know her every move.

They had dated a year before he asked her dad if he could marry her. Her parents loved Joe. They thought that Joe treated Brooke like a princess because she hid the bad from them. Each year the arguments and demeaning comments increased. She never shared that with her parents.

When planning the wedding, Joe even suggested buying property in her hometown. She should be close to her family, he would say. They had bought their now 25-acre lot and built her dream home, which Joe was never crazy about.

She wanted cozy and comfortable, not luxurious and unlivable. To compromise, he built himself a dream garage far from the house. His excuse was so he didn't have to see the "small redneck house" that she had designed.

Looking back, she never could figure out why he wanted to live here close to her family. She now understood that he saw it as a way to isolate her from the world, being so far out in the country.

As the years passed, small disagreements would get blown into massive fights. Brooke told Shirley that she usually didn't even know what the arguments were about. She would eventually blow up at Joe after he had been yelling and cussing at her for an hour or more.

By the next morning, Joe would have turned it around and blamed her, saying it was her fault. He would tell her he couldn't believe the things she had said to him. She would be shocked and spent years trying to convince him that wasn't what happened. Eventually, she stopped fighting it.

Looking back, she realized those were the nights that he took longer in the garage than normal. He was drinking. He had two sides to him, regular Joe and drunk Joe, and she didn't care for either of them. She knew it made her look weak, but she couldn't win. He often made her question her own words, and she accepted much of the blame.

When she was thirty-two, and Frankie was a one year old, her sweet daddy passed away. Her heart was crushed. It was a pain she could never put into words. She was a daddy's girl and loved him more than anyone in the world except her Frankie. She and Joe had been married for nine years then.

After her dad passed away, things changed even more with Joe. His anger towards her increased, and somehow, this made him feel like he completely controlled her now. He would say that he was glad he no longer had to share her. She was his.

The week of her daddy's death, Joe was cold and numb to her pain. He wouldn't help her with any part of the process. He didn't even help care for Frankie. She had the weight of the world on her and the most pain she had ever known.

She remembered how intensely spiteful Joe had been that week. Even on the night of her father's death, she tried to wake Joe up and asked him to hold her, as she hurt so badly. He started cussing and yelling that it was fucking four in the morning. She just rolled over, grabbed her pillow, and cried.

That next morning, she had taken Frankie to Shirley's house, and when she returned home to pick up Joe, he was gone. She had to leave in order to make their appointment. She picked up her mom and headed to the funeral home to finalize the arrangements.

Joe showed up drunk and was mad that she had left without him. Even her mom commented on how mean Joe was being to Brooke and how unaffected he seemed by her father's death.

Brooke wanted her dad's funeral handled with the utmost care and respect. Her daddy deserved that. He had been such a strong and loving man. When she was in high school, she remembered the boys were scared to look at her, fearing what her daddy would say to them. He was a large confident man that made people look and admire him. At 6'5", he made a statement just walking into a room.

To Brooke, her daddy was a gentle giant. She had cried almost every day since his death, wishing she could talk to him just one more time. Her daddy had taken care of his family and loved them very much. He was a great father and husband. She used to think he had set the bar too high, and maybe that's why she had excused Joe's bad behavior.

Shortly after her daddy's death, Brooke's mom was diagnosed with MS. Everything happened very fast and the debilitating disease progressed quickly, and she needed full-time care. Her mother was no longer able to walk or do things for herself.

Joe paid to have a live-in nurse move in with Brooke's mother and has continued to pay for the last ten years. A fact that he reminds her of every day. Due to the high cost of treatments and live-in nursing care, she knew she couldn't do it without him. Joe's money keeps her mother alive, but he was slowly killing Brooke with his actions. Now looking over at him in his recliner, she fumed at his insensitivity.

Brooke got up and walked over to the window. Due to the three inches of snow from the storm, there would be no school or work today. She knew their road wouldn't be cleared anytime soon or not at all. Hopefully, the sun would help melt it off.

Brooke made her coffee and headed to her front porch. This was her happy place. She found peace on the porch. She enjoyed looking out at the land and all the natural beauties that God had put there for them. Obviously, she didn't mind having the days off with Frankie, but the thought of being snowed in with Joe gave her anxiety.

Frankie followed her out and sat in the swing with her.

"Mom, can we please ride the four-wheelers today?"

"Yes, of course! Isn't the snow beautiful?" Brooke responded with as much excitement as Frankie had.

He nodded and popped up from the swing. "Yes! Can I get dressed and go play in it now?"

She laughed at his eagerness but agreed he could go play after he ate. The screen door slammed as he headed in. She shook her head and smiled.

She had texted her boss earlier to let her know she would be out until at least the following Monday. She loved her job but would enjoy the next few days off. When Frankie started pre-k, she had gone back to work but was thankful she had been able to be home to watch all of his firsts.

Brooke and Frankie had spent most days at her mom's house, during those early years. Joe always expected dinner on the table when he got home from work, so they would have to leave in time to get everything prepared. Joe usually found reasons to complain about what she had or hadn't cooked.

Now all these years later, working and parenting had become easier for her. She was good at her job and always took care of her family.

She was so good that her company always used her as their spokesperson for the November Sales Rally. She enjoyed the rallies because it gave her a break from her normal everyday duties.

This year the rally had been packed with so many new people as well as the one person that had blown her away. When she ran into Tom, it was so unexpected. He was a breath of fresh air.

They were both shocked and happy to see each other. It was easy to chat and catch up. Their ease of conversation made it seem like no time had passed.

Tom had even brought up her dad's passing and apologized for missing his funeral, as he had been in Texas that week. He knew his parents had attended the funeral to show their respect and wished he could have also been there.

They spent all their free time together for the remainder of the long weekend and have continued to see each other since.

Now sipping her coffee, she sat confused and afraid. Her thoughts turned back to the night before. She had been at the park where the murders had occurred. Somewhere she shouldn't have been, doing something she shouldn't have been doing.

Brooke despised cheaters and she believed they only hurt people. She thought it should be simple. If you want to cheat with someone, step up and just break up with the person you are with. However, she knew that she was stuck with Joe. How had she let herself get caught up in these new emotions with Tom? He was soft-spoken and kind. Tom was handsome in a rugged way while Joe looked manicured.

Her mind was going in a thousand different directions. Cold chills ran down her spine as she realized she could have been killed last night at the park. She thought about the man she had seen in her rearview mirror. Was the man she saw the killer? Could he have been one of the victims? She didn't know where he had even come from. Her view had been blurred by the rain and sleet, but also by her nerves.

He could have been running to her car for help. Anxiety started to build in her mind. She willed herself to reflect back on her surroundings, but honestly, she wasn't even sure which vehicles were still parked around her.

Brooke knew she needed to talk to Tom. The reporter said that the police were asking anyone with any information to let them know immediately. She knew firsthand that the park did not have cameras. Tom had assured her of that before the first time they met.

Based on what she had seen, she knew she had to tell the cops about the man in her mirror. She really couldn't tell them much, except he seemed tall and was wearing an orange toboggan.

Brooke wondered, who was he, and did he know who she was?

Chapter 3

MEANWHILE, THE DOWNTOWN AREA was a disaster. TV Stations had vans parked everywhere. The town had never seen so much traffic and activity.

Tom and his family were watching everything on TV as well. He assumed the police were frantically working. Tom's house sat just across the street from the town square. It was a big historical house built in the late 1800s.

The news reporter said the names of the victims would be released soon in a press statement from the Police Chief. She continued talking about the community and its history.

Tom looked over at his girls, and they both were staring at their phones. They would live on those phones at fourteen and fifteen years old if he let them. The girls were reading out loud all the posts and comments that the locals were posting on social media.

Even the bakery owner from downtown had been interviewed by one of the television stations. The clip had played at least twenty times. The baker was a nice old gentleman who just liked being in the center of everything. He and his wife had served on the town's board for the last 40 years. They were good people, just tended to be very nosey. According to his statement, the baker wasn't even at the park.

Tom couldn't believe a murder had happened here in his hometown. This was a safe town. He thought about the previous night. Brooke was a light to his life when things had been so dark. She had made him feel alive again. Guilt consumed his thoughts as he looked over at his wife. He hated what he was doing, as he knew it would devastate her if she knew about the affair.

His wife, Amy, sat quietly beside the girls. Over the last year, she had become a homebody. She never wanted to leave the house. She would never leave if she didn't have to chauffer the girls around. Tom had watched her go from being shy to withdrawn and easily frightened.

She had been depressed for the last year or so. They had visited a few counselors, but Amy seemed to have no desire to get better. She had even started doing pickup orders online for their groceries to avoid going into the grocery store.

"Can I get you some more coffee, honey?" He asked her, seeing that she was nervous from the news about a murder in town.

"I'm okay. I will get some in a bit." She answered but never made eye contact with him.

Tom wanted to grab and hold her, but he knew she would just push him away. There was a wall between them that he didn't understand. He wasn't sure how to explain what he felt for Brooke. He knew it wasn't the kind of love he felt for Amy.

He had been over the moon for Amy from the beginning of their junior year in high school. Just the sight of Amy had made his heart race. Seeing her now and how weak she had become made his heart ache. He had tried to reassure her that she was safe and that he would always protect her.

He was ashamed of his actions with Brooke, but seeing her gave him a feeling of joy again. At home, it felt like he was walking on eggshells, and being with Brooke had given him a break from that feeling. Things had been so good with Amy until this last year. She was battling internally with her own mind. He couldn't do anything but offer her encouragement.

As he watched her fidget with her phone, he thought about her past. Amy's childhood had been horrible. Amy's dad had been in prison on and off for selling drugs since she was five years old. After her father had first gone to jail, Amy's mom had moved from man to man, from relationship to relationship. Her mother never had the strength to make it alone as a single parent.

Amy had taken a lot of beatings from some of those men. The local Department of Family and Child Services had actually been called several times, but they had no proof, as Amy would claim she had fallen. Thankfully though, Amy claimed that none of them had violated her.

Amy started working when she was sixteen years old to help her mom with bills and to save enough money to eventually get herself out of her situation. One week into her senior year, her mom packed up and took off. Leaving nothing but a note that read: **The rent is paid for two more weeks. I love you, but I can't do this anymore**. Amy was crushed and heartbroken but hid her pain. Amy was able to stay with friends until they graduated. She had moved in with Tom's parents after Tom left for college.

During college, Tom worked to save as much money as possible. They were together every free moment they could make. By his junior year, he proposed to Amy, and they had started planning their wedding. Amy was able to work at the local antique store and save as well. She wasn't interested in going to college. She just wanted to make money and save so she never had to live broke again.

Surprisingly, when the girls were born, Amy had been the most amazing mother. She had been so attentive and loving with the girls. Lucy and Addy both adored their mom.

Tom knew the girls had noticed that their mom had changed over the last year, but neither understood what was happening. Sometimes they would ask him questions about their mom. Both would mention incidents where Amy had panicked and raced them back home from wherever they were. Unfortunately, he never knew how to respond.

Looking over at the girls now, he realized how much they both looked like their mother. Lucy, the oldest, was feisty and extremely smart. Addy was gentle and caring, always trying to help everyone. The girls were really close, and they acted like twins even though they were a year apart. They were unlike your typical dramatic teenage girls and he knew he had been blessed.

Suddenly, as he watched them, Addy shushed the room and pointed at the TV.

"Look, Dad, the Chief is about to speak!" Addy shouted excitedly.

Tom grabbed the remote control and turned up the volume on the television. He prayed this would be over quickly for everyone involved and that it wasn't something crazy, like a serial killer.

The thought of three people shot less than five minutes from his home, and where he and Brooke had been, unnerved him.

Tom had also thought a lot about Eric today, since seeing him on the television. They had been like brothers growing up and were still close friends, although he hadn't confided in Eric about Brooke. Tom was scared that Eric would hate him for it. He couldn't imagine how Eric felt finding a dead woman.

The Chief walked out and stood at a podium set up in front of the station. He cleared his throat and was visibly nervous.

"Good morning. This is the saddest day of my career. Seeing this kind of thing happen anywhere is horrible, but for it to happen here in our town is devastating. This is a town that loves, not kills." The Chief paused as he spoke.

"I would like to express my sympathy to the families of the deceased. We are working hard to discover what happened to these victims and who the perpetrator is. For now, we will not be releasing any information about the murders, but we will release the names of the victims."

Some of the reporters started shouting questions from the crowd that had gathered. "Chief, do you have any leads or suspects yet?"

"As I just stated, I will not be giving any details of the murders at this time."

"Do you suspect a serial killer?" Another reporter asked.

"At this time, I do not. The investigation will be our top priority, and we hope to have this solved quickly. We are asking anyone who has any information or was at the park last night to please contact our office. The department will make sure that we catch the person responsible."

The crowd started chatting amongst themselves.

"Ladies and gentlemen of the community, you should not be afraid. Our department will do everything we can to protect you," the Chief continued.

He then released the names "Ray Harper from the metro area of Georgia, and Husband and Wife, Terry and Julie Parker of Texas."

Tom's mouth dropped as he stared at the television.

"Oh my God!" Tom shouted.

He knew two of the victims, and he knew them well. Terry was his business partner. Shock filled Tom. His heart was racing. How could this be possible?

He and Terry had attended the same university and had remained friends. About fourteen years prior, Terry had contacted him wanting to start a software company. As they chatted about the details, Tom remembered his excitement. They decided that they would each contribute fifty percent of the startup cost.

Tom had taken out a second mortgage for his half and sold some land his grandfather had left him. Once things had progressed over the next six months, Terry had admitted that he had borrowed some of his half of the money from his father-in-law.

Terry had told Tom not to worry about the money he had borrowed as it would not affect the company. Tom had been concerned about another person being involved with the business, but his lawyers said it would not affect the contract. He wanted to trust Terry but also knew to be cautious to make sure the contract was concrete.

The business had grown and become very successful. In the company's early years, Tom sacrificed a lot of his time but could now work from home and be with his family, except when traveling.

His sales position required him to travel some, plus the company was based in Texas. Terry handled the office duties and managed the employees, while Tom dealt with the sales side remotely. Tom only needed to visit the office a few times a year.

Tom couldn't think clearly, but he knew that he needed to contact his office and get a handle on things there. His mind was racing with thoughts.

Tom heard crying and looked over at Amy. His heart ached for her. She was taking this harder than he expected.

Tom excused himself from the room. This was a tragedy. He needed to make some calls, so he headed to his home office. Amy watched him leave the room. She sat dazed as her thoughts focused on one thing. This was the reason she didn't leave the house.

The girls followed Tom to his office. They recognized the Parkers' names and started asking questions.

Addy, the youngest, asked, "Dad, what were they doing at the park?"

Tom shook his head as he answered. "I didn't even know they were here in Willowville."

Lucy was crying now as well. "This is so sad. Do you think it is a serial killer?"

"No honey, I don't think so. I think if the Chief thought we were in danger, he would have warned us."

"What will happen to your business now?" Addy questioned him.

He told them he didn't have any answers, but he reassured them that everything would be ok. Although in his mind, he was asking all those same questions.

When the girls left the room, he reached for his phone. He pulled up Eric's contact and hit call. He wasn't even sure if Eric could take calls with everything going on right now. Eric answered with a shaky voice.

"Tom, can you believe this shit!"

"Dude, I can't imagine how you are feeling! Damn, I was blown away from just hearing about it. Then to know you found the body was unthinkable."

"It was a scene from a horror movie. I went outside and noticed someone lying on the ground. I raced over, thinking whoever it was had slipped on the sleet."

Eric paused.

"Damn, I am so sorry." Tom hurt, feeling his pain.

"The body was face down. There was so much blood. When I rolled the body over, all I could see was the bullet exit hole in the forehead. And then..." Eric's voice trailed off.

"Then I realized it was Julie." He finally said.

"Oh shit, I didn't even think about that. I was so caught up with everything that I forgot you knew Julie."

"Yeah, I really don't know how I knew it was her because it was so gruesome."

Tom tried to comfort him and told him they would meet soon.

"There's one other thing, Tom. I didn't tell the Chief that I recognized Julie."

Before Tom could ask him why, Eric ended the call abruptly.

Tom felt terrible for Eric. He hadn't even thought about him recognizing Julie. Eric had traveled with Tom to Texas several times over the years.

Tom then dialed the number for his corporate office.

Chapter 4

SATURDAY EVENING, BROOKE SAT on her porch watching Frankie play in the snow. They had spent most of the last couple of days riding four-wheelers and building snow people.

Although three inches isn't much snow, it was enough to have fun in. She warned Frankie his wet clothes would make him sick, so he changed several times. She would have two loads of laundry just from his snow clothes, but she didn't mind. She was happy to have this long weekend off.

They had ridden all over the property for hours. She wasn't sure how Frankie still had any energy left. He had been going to bed late and waking up so early. Brooke was exhausted.

Frankie asked some questions a few times about the town murders, but luckily the snow had distracted him enough to keep him busy. Joe hadn't joined them very much. He had come out a few times, mostly to scold them about how crazy they were and that it was just snow. He spent most of his time off down in his garage.

She hoped that she would be able to get herself out of the house by morning. She wanted to go visit her mom. She also knew she needed to contact Tom. It had been too risky for both her and Tom to contact each other these last few days.

She saw on the news that the names of the victims had been released. It seemed they were all from out of town. She felt so sorry for their families. She knew how terrible the loss of a loved one felt and couldn't imagine how much harder it would be to lose someone because of such evil. The Chief had given a statement and ended it with a request that if anyone had been to the park that night or knew any details, to please contact them.

The Chief had been friends with her mom and dad. Brooke knew how hard all of this was for him. He loved this town as if it was his child. She knew that she and Tom needed to let the Chief know that they had been at the park. Also, she would need to tell them about the man in her rearview mirror. When she saw pictures of the victims, their faces didn't seem familiar, but weirdly she had a strange feeling that he wasn't one of the murdered men.

Her phone rang just as Frankie passed by to change clothes again. It was Shirley.

"Hey!" Brooke answered.

Because of the storm, Shirley had lost power at her house until today, and so they had not talked since Tuesday. No power for Shirley meant no Wi-Fi and no phone service, as she lived so far out in the country. Shirley was going on about how she just couldn't believe a murder had happened in their town.

"I was so worried about you, Brooke. Do you think you were there when it happened?"

"I don't think so, but I honestly have no idea." Brooke then told her about dropping her phone and having to go back for it.

"Then, I started to leave again and there was a man in my rearview mirror. I don't know who he was, as I couldn't see very well. He just seemed tall and was wearing an orange toboggan. I panicked and hit the gas."

"Holy crap! That would have scared the shit out of me!" Shirley blurted.

"It scared me for different reasons. I was scared someone recognized me, and I was going to be busted." Brooke replied.

"Speaking of being busted, how did things go for you and Tom that night?"

Shirley knew everything about Brooke's life. They had no secrets from each other. They gave each other support through everything, including the good, the bad, and the ugly. Shirley knew that Brooke wasn't a person that would intentionally hurt anyone. They had been best friends since kindergarten.

Shirley was divorced and had one son. Their boys were only about a month apart in age. Shirley's ex-husband had decided to cheat on her about five years earlier. He had met a woman online and left Shirley. He paid child support every week, but he didn't use any visitation time with Reece.

Even though Brooke was still married, they shared their children's needs to help each other out as much as possible. The boys took turns sleeping over at each other's houses.

Shirley despised Joe. She knew why Brooke stayed but wished he would disappear. Brooke was her only family, as her parents had died years ago. Both ladies leaned on each other for strength.

Brooke blushed as she told Shirley every detail of her and Tom's time together.

"It was incredible! We did it!" Brooke laughed at herself.

Shirley busted out laughing as well.

"I guess that was a terrible choice of words! I was blown away! It felt so special. We talked, and then he pulled me close to him."

She paused, "Now I sort of feel like an idiot as we were in the backseat. It was like I was seventeen again making out in the back of a car. Real romantic, right?"

Shirley was still chuckling. "I'm sorry, Brooke. I am not laughing at you. I LOVE it!"

"I was glowing until I saw the man in my rearview mirror. Then I got all in my head. But it gets even better, when I got halfway home, I realized I was almost out of gas! I had to go back to town! Oh, and I almost slid off the road by the time I started back to the house."

Shirley was now crying from laughing so hard. "Girl, you are a bull in a china shop!"

Brooke was so happy to talk to Shirley, because she always made Brooke feel better.

"I just wish I didn't feel so guilty!" she confessed.

"I am so happy for you. You needed that! I just worry about you getting caught. Joe would try to take everything away from you, that stupid bastard."

"Yeah, well now I am scared Joe's gonna find out, because I have to go tell the Chief that I was at the park."

Shirley disagreed. "I think you need to wait and talk to Tom before you do anything. That way, you are both on the same page. Honestly, Brooke, you guys being there or not isn't going to have anything to do with solving the murders!"

"How did Joe react to you getting home so late?"

"Thankfully, everyone was sleeping by the time I got home. I was grateful for that because it saved me from an argument." Brooke thought about the last couple of days as she spoke.

"Oddly enough though, Joe has actually been really weird these last couple of days. He was ugly the morning after, but since then, he's been very quiet."

"Oh sorry, I forgot to ask you something. I am taking Reece to play indoor golf tomorrow – do you and Frankie want to go with us?" Shirley interrupted.

"I can't go – I have too much that I need to get done." Brooke explained.

"Well, how about if I take Frankie with us? Would you mind? The boys would love it."

"That would be perfect. I really need to go get some groceries and visit my mom. Frankie has eaten everything in the house. But what about you guys staying for dinner after you get back?"

"Yes, that sounds great. It will save me from having to stop on the way back home." Shirley replied.

When they hung up, Brooke was still smiling. She was so thankful for Shirley. The boys would be able to keep playing, and Joe would be on good behavior since company would be at the house.

She should have been at the grocery store the night of the murders, and she wouldn't be in this position now. She didn't mind leaving Frankie at home with Joe usually, but since everything that had happened, she felt better that Frankie would be with Shirley away from the house.

Joe was calmer around Frankie but didn't spend much time with him. Brooke knew that Frankie had seen the ugly side of Joe. He had made a comment last year that his teacher was getting a divorce, and he understood that sometimes it just had to happen. Frankie informed her that if she ever divorced his dad, he would understand. She had brushed the conversation off because of everything going on with her mother. Divorce was not an option. She wouldn't be able to explain that to a child.

She started making her to-do list on her phone. First, she would go visit her mom, then go to the grocery store, and lastly, she would try to reach out to Tom. She had missed seeing her mom these last several days. She also missed the days when her mom was able to go out shopping with her.

She finally called for Frankie to come in, playtime was over. It was now bedtime.

On Sunday morning, Brooke stood in the kitchen looking out the window. It was so beautiful to look out at the trees and the open spaces. The snow had melted away somewhat.

She always loved Sundays because it gave her more time at home. She spent a lot of time, when she was home, out on her porch relaxing and watching the deer come through her yard. Each time, it made her smile. Seeing the deer always reminded her of her daddy.

Her daddy had loved hunting. Every year he had looked forward to hunting season. The deer now gave Brooke pleasure seeing them playing instead of being on the dinner table like when she was growing up. She had gone hunting with her father when she was younger but had never actually shot anything other than cans.

She knew Shirley should be here soon to pick up Frankie. Brooke planned on heading to town as soon as they left. The refrigerator was almost empty. Frankie could eat as much as two grown men.

Once Shirley arrived, they couldn't chat much as the boys stayed close by to them. Brooke waved as they left, and then she headed to her room to get dressed. Entering the bedroom, she met Joe. He was looking at her with disgust.

"Where are you headed off to?" Joe questioned her.

Brooke shook her head as she thought about all the times Joe had accused her of cheating. She almost got a little joy out of knowing that she was finally doing what he had been accusing her of forever, but mostly guilt filled her as it was something she wasn't proud of. All the years of accusations, and now he would be right.

"I am just going to visit my mom and grab some groceries. Frankie has depleted our cupboards." She tried to manage a smile, just wishing him to be kind.

"I thought you just bought groceries?"

She raised her eyes to his as her body tensed.

"That was almost a week ago, Joe. You know how much Frankie eats. We've all eaten more being stuck here at the house."

Joe mumbled something, but Brooke was unsure what it was.

Now in the bedroom, she quickly dressed and prayed the roads would allow her to get out. Shirley had told her they seemed pretty good, but Brooke was still nervous as she wasn't comfortable driving in ice or snow.

Brooke drove slowly to her mother's house. Her mom greeted her with a big hello. Brooke noticed her mom seemed to be having a good day. The neurologist had started her on a new treatment a few months prior, and it appeared to be working.

Her mom came out on the porch and walked herself from the door to the porch swing using her cane. Brooke was excited, as it was the first time that she had seen her mom walk that far with a cane since she had first been diagnosed. Brooke chatted with her mom and Mary, the live-in nurse.

Brooke told her mom about Frankie's adventures over the last couple of days in the snow. She told her about the snowmen they had built together. They both laughed. For the first time in several years, Brooke thought maybe there was hope for her mother to be a little healthier. It gave her such joy. Brooke would love it if her mother got to leave the house for more than just doctors' appointments.

A few hours later, Brooke pulled into the Calico Mart, the only grocery store in town. She wanted to skip across the parking lot, thinking about how great it was to see her mom in less pain. She noticed the lot still had snow in several areas.

Pulling out her grocery list, she scooted her cart around the store. She gathered up the stuff to make a big pot of chili.

She loaded up on snacks and drinks. As she was going up and down the aisles, she spoke to a few people that she passed. She tried to keep it short because all of them wanted to talk about the murders. Just the mention of the park made her anxious.

After she was done gathering up her groceries, she headed to the checkout line. She was struggling to get her card to scan, but as usual, the chip rarely scanned on the first try. She made a mental note to order a new card. Just as she finally got it to work and started to enter her pin number, she looked up as the cashier was saying something about the murders.

Her gaze went up to the aisle at the other end from where she was standing. There stood a very tall man with an orange toboggan. She immediately recognized this was the man from the night of the murders! He was the man that was in her rearview mirror.

Brooke finished checking out and raced out of the store, totally ignoring the cashier, who was still chatting. She almost knocked a woman down as she raced her buggy out the door.

Brooke apologized but did not stop. "I'm so sorry."

Once at her car, she was throwing groceries in as fast as she could while watching the door of the store. She didn't see the man exit, although she may have missed him. She left the cart sitting right by the car.

She locked the car doors and drove off. The way the man had looked at her made chills run down her spine. Brooke was in panic mode. She had no idea who the man was. He was not a local, and he certainly was not murdered. She needed to contact the police. But she was too afraid to go to the police station. Right now, she just wanted to get home, away from town. She watched her rearview mirror, expecting to see his face again.

Eric Stinson stood now watching Brooke as she drove away. He had followed her around the store but stayed an aisle over to avoid being seen. Then she had nearly knocked a woman over on her quick exit out the door.

He wondered if she had seen or noticed him, and that's why she ran out so quickly. This last week had been insane. He was now standing in the Calico Mart parking lot, near his car. He thought about Brooke, and she had always been one of the nicest girls in town. He was older than her but had hung around her crowd a whole lot when they were young.

Eric smiled, thinking of Brooke's best friend, Shirley. He had loved Shirley back in their younger years. He had seen Brooke several times over the last month, coming and going almost once a week from the park. He had seen her car parked the night of the murders. His mind filled with anger as he thought about that night.

He wanted to contact Brooke, but he knew that would look odd. He wanted to know why she had been meeting with Tom. He knew they were both married. His mom had told him that Brooke wasn't happily married, according to the talk of the town.

He couldn't imagine Tom cheating on his wife though. Amy had been having some problems, but that didn't change the fact they were married. He was close to Tom, but he was still upset with him.

Eric had never had children, even though he had always wanted them. So instead, since life had thrown him a curve ball, he just enjoyed working at the County Rec Department with all the kids. Those kids treated him like family. Now, he started to load his groceries into the car. He was filled with anger again as he thought that some of those kids could have been hurt the night of the murders.

Eric pulled out his phone. He had Brooke's phone number from a few years ago, when he had helped coach her son's basketball team. He hit the phone call button before he could stop himself.

"Hello," Brooke answered on the third ring. He hung up.

He thought about the times he had seen Brooke climbing into Tom's SUV. It had disappointed him. He had respected them both so much. But now, he had lost that respect, because they both had children. He had even coached Tom's girls throughout several of the last years.

Eric looked at his contacts. There was the number he wanted to dial, but he didn't have the nerve. For almost ten years, he had wanted to hit send for this contact, but he had talked himself out of it every time. He now closed his phone and headed home.

When Brooke arrived home, she was shaking. She had received a call on the way home, but the number had shown up as unknown, and then the caller had hung up. It made her even more nervous. She started to put away the groceries. Who in the world was the man from the park? Had he followed her to the store? It didn't feel like a coincidence.

Now, she had only a few hours before Frankie would be back home. Shirley had called and said the boys were having a blast. She told Shirley that something had happened at the grocery store.

"I'm positive that I saw mirror man," Brooke exclaimed.

"Oh damn, Brooke. Did he say anything to you?" Shirley asked with concern.

"No, he was in the checkout line on the opposite side of the registers. He just stared at me. I didn't even see him come out of the store! It creeped me out. I know that was the man I saw in my rearview mirror."

Shirley mentioned that the boys had been chatting and asking a lot of questions about the murder. She had tried to keep them distracted and on a different subject.

Brooke was still shaking as she was stirring her pot of homemade chili. She was afraid. Luckily, Joe was still in his garage. He spent so much time in there and, if she was honest, that was a great thing to her. She jumped when the door burst open with the boys running in. Shirley came in laughing and immediately stopped when she looked at Brooke.

"I'm okay. It just freaked me out. I know it was him."

"Well, he is probably new to town, and just happened to be going to his car that night at the same time."

"It just felt like he was purposely watching me that night and yet I couldn't see his face."

She started fixing bowls of chili and set out crackers, cheese, and sour cream. The boys came back into the kitchen, so they stopped chatting. She still seemed shaky when they sat down at the table. Shirley was worried about her.

Dinner went by with no additional drama. Brooke was ridden with anxiety. She tried to control her emotions though, for the boys' sakes. Both boys were telling Joe all about how well they had done golfing. Joe seemed like he enjoyed their chatter.

"Oh Dad, guess what? I hit a hole-in-one."

Joe said, "Of course you did, because any son of mine will excel at anything he does."

The next few hours flew by with all the details about the day. Frankie brought up the murders after he finished eating. He said he was scared. Joe surprised Brooke because he had kindly told Frankie not to worry. He would always protect him. She wished he could be that way with her. Joe seemed more chatty than normal, with her, and with Shirley as well.

Chapter 5

A COUPLE OF DAYS following the murders, Tom was sitting at the conference table in the corporate office in Texas. He still couldn't believe Terry and Julie were dead.

Tom was there to meet with John, the Chief Financial Officer, and the company's attorney, Steve Jennings. Tom trusted them both completely. They had been with the company since the beginning and had seen Tom and Terry through all of the ups and downs of running a business. He considered them both friends, as well as associates.

Now sitting around the table, they all were still in shock.

"Thanks for meeting with me so quickly. This is unbelievable! I don't even know where to begin." Tom paused as his emotions were uncontrollable. "It's so insane. I can't believe they are dead!"

"We didn't even know until you called us. Terry has been out of the office since Thursday of last week, and his calendar showed he was taking off for personal days. No one from the family has even contacted us, yet." John reported.

"I didn't even know they were in Willowville! Did either of you know that they were coming to Georgia?" Tom asked. "They usually stay with Amy and me when they are in town or passing through. I can't imagine what they were doing there without my knowledge. Do either of you know Ray Harper, the other victim? I don't recognize that name."

"It's definitely odd, and I don't know who Ray Harper is. Murdered? My God!" John answered.

"I just don't understand any of this," Steve exclaimed. "None of it makes sense."

"I am at a loss on what needs to happen and how to keep everything in the company going. It's a shame to say, but I've been so focused on sales and busy doing my part of the business that I hadn't been concerned with anything else." Tom confessed.

"We understand. Why would you have been concerned that something like this would ever happen? The first thing we need to do is to set up a plan." Steve advised.

"Let's start with assuring all of the employees that their jobs are secure, for now. We will continue as usual while we figure out how we are moving forward." Tom advised John.

"I have reviewed the Business Incorporation Contract, regarding the partnership, and it is very clear. It reads that if either partner dies, the surviving partner would then control three-quarters of the company and have the option to buy the remaining quarter at today's market value. We will need an outside consulting firm to run an audit to determine the company value." Steve explained.

"Let's reconvene later this afternoon." Tom told them.

By the time they were done, Tom was starving. He realized he hadn't eaten since on the way to the airport at four that morning. He jumped in the company car that his business had on hand.

Speaking to John and Steve today had eased his mind somewhat.

The ringing phone ended that feeling. He answered quickly.

"Hey, Tom, it's John."

"I wanted to let you know that one of the senior accountants just advised me that Terry had previously ordered an internal audit, and we expect the report to be ready later today. I wasn't aware of it earlier when we spoke because Terry had requested it privately."

"Is that normal? Do you normally run internal audits randomly?" Tom questioned.

"No, usually the reports are run annually around tax time. I've never seen it requested like this before. I did call Steve and advised him of the situation."

After driving through a burger joint, he returned to the office and waited in the conference room. The office wasn't large, but they did employ about 100 people. Over half of the employees worked remotely from their homes. He looked around and admired the office.

He normally enjoyed his trips to the office. He always chatted with everyone. He knew all the employees' names and most of their families' names. It meant something to him. He really cared about all of them. Amy, years earlier, said she had no idea how his brain held so much information. The staff was surprised by how well he remembered such details about their lives.

Tom smiled briefly, thinking of those years. It turned to sadness when he thought of Terry's family. Even Amy had been so upset when he said he had to fly out here. She didn't want him to leave, and she seemed so scared.

John, Steve, and one of the senior accountants came into the room and joined him.

"I have looked over the recent audit, and something is wrong. We found some discrepancies. Money is missing." The senior accountant advised them.

"What the hell do you mean missing money? How did we lose money?" Tom frantically responded.

The senior accountant continued to explain. "There are transactions showing money was moved, but the audit couldn't determine where or why. We are investigating it and should be able to explain more by tomorrow."

They ended the meeting and planned on another early start in the morning. Tom just wanted to go back to his hotel room. He wanted to check in with his family.

He was still worried about Brooke as well. He hadn't been able to contact her out of fear that her husband might be with her. They had no secret codes for communicating. He realized they were terrible cheaters, as they didn't have a plan. He laughed at that thought- he wasn't good at cheating, which was a good thing.

After checking in at his hotel room, he stretched across the bed. He was so tired. He called Amy, and she answered right away.

"Tom, are you on your way home?" she asked.

"No honey, you know that I was planning on flying back Monday afternoon, but now it may be a few days longer."

She was pouting. He could hear it over the phone.

"I have some extra stuff to take care of." He explained to Amy.

"Is something else going on?" Amy asked, and Tom could hear the fear in her voice.

"No, nothing else is going on. Everything is fine. I just need to ensure everything with the business is running smoothly here before I leave." He frowned as he lied to her.

"Are the girls okay, sweetheart?" Tom tried to change the subject.

"The girls cried and begged to go over to your parents' house, and now I'm home alone. I will be okay, and I promise to call you if I need anything. Worst case, I can stay with the girls at your parent's house if I need to."

He chatted a bit longer with her and tried to reassure her that she was safe.

"I love you, Amy. I really think these murders are random and the killer has probably moved on. You just need to focus on yourself and the girls. Everything is going to be fine. I just want to finish here so I don't have to return anytime soon."

"Okay. I will try. I just wish you could take care of things from here. I love you." Amy hung up the phone.

He still couldn't figure out why Terry was in Willowville. He tried again to remember if Terry had ever mentioned Ray Harper. Terry was a talker, and Tom would sometimes drift off when he was rattling about things.

The next few days didn't go any better for Tom. If anything, they were worse. The accounting team had been trying to trace the missing money. They had found three withdrawal transfers to an offshore account, but they were still waiting on more details.

Tom was furious and puzzled. At this point, he couldn't imagine who in his company would be stealing. His mind went to the worst-case scenario that he could imagine, what if Terry had been the one stealing, and could this have something to do with his death?

John had called him this morning requesting he come in immediately to meet with him and Steve, as it was urgent.

Tom's nerves were shot. His life was usually uneventful. Following the announcement of Terry and Julie's murder in his hometown, everything had changed. From worrying about his family, Brooke, the business, and now this missing money, his mind was exhausted. He didn't know that this meeting would be the one that changed everything.

John greeted him but seemed very disappointed. "Tom, we have some disturbing news."

"Tom, against my better judgment, I am handling this differently than I normally would," Steve explained.

Tom was confused as he watched Steve's face as he spoke.

"This will be the only meeting that I can keep off the record. My advice to you is hire an attorney for yourself quickly."

"What in the hell do I need an attorney for? What are you talking about?" Tom yelled loud enough to be heard outside the conference room.

John stood up, walked over, and sat by Tom. His words seemed to echo. "The accounting team has been able to trace the offshore account. The missing money is in a Swiss bank, under the name THOMAS ADCOCK. "

Silence filled the air. Tom was stunned. Steve spoke first.

"Normally, under these circumstances, the police would have to be involved, but John and I feel like something is off. We both think the world of you, and we trust that this must be a mistake. It is a mistake, right?"

"Of course, it's a fucking mistake!"

"I am sorry, but I had to ask! We will give you a few weeks to figure this out before reporting anything." Steve replied.

Tom's head rested in his hands. He wanted to scream and tell them this was crazy, but he was too confused to argue. Both John and Steve left the room.

Tom remained sitting in the conference room. He was trying to wrap his mind around everything he had just heard. An offshore account in his name was impossible. It wasn't true. He knew nothing about this kind of stuff. He was good at managing his finances, but this was something he had only seen in movies. His assistant, Tammy, came into the room with coffee. She sat down. She had worked for him since the business started.

Tom confided in her and explained what was happening.

"It's not true, and you would think, as an owner of a software company, I would know how to prove it."

"You will figure it out, Tom. I know you wouldn't steal from your own company."

Tammy thought about the years that she had been a single mom, and Tom had always gone above and beyond to help her. One year, his family bought Christmas presents for both her boys.

Tom tried to reassure her, and maybe himself, that he would figure this out. He needed to find out everything he could.

Fear started to settle in. This had to be connected in some way with the murders. Would people now think that he had killed Terry? He immediately contacted his family attorney.

Now back home in Georgia, Tom was waiting on his back porch, reflecting on the week in Texas.

He was stuck impatiently waiting for news from his attorney as well as waiting for news from his company. He had to get this settled. He asked his attorney if he should contact the Chief and let him know that Terry was his business partner or wait until he knew what was happening. The attorney had advised him to wait. Tom decided that he would hold off. For now, he was going to spend any free time he had with Amy and the girls.

He would also wait a few more days and then text Brooke. They needed to talk as soon as possible. Tom couldn't believe all that was happening around him and how fast it was happening.

Chapter 6

THE CHIEF SAT AT his desk with his hands covering his face. He still couldn't believe what had happened in his town. The case was far from being solved. He had assigned a department just to work the tip line as it was overwhelmed with calls. Several calls were from people that had been at the park the night of the murders, but mostly bogus calls from people that lived in the community trying to be detectives.

The Chief had only assigned two sergeants to work directly on the case. They needed to keep things totally confidential as they worked through the details. Sergeant Smith was working the crime scene for tire tracks, footprints, or any other leads that might help find the suspect. Sergeant Nally was tasked with gathering detailed information on each of the victims.

The county employee, Eric, was certain that no gunshot noises were heard, so they assumed the shooter may have used a gun with a suppressor. The interviews with Eric had been intense, as he had helped determine the shooting timeline.

They concluded the suspect was most likely a marksman, as each victim had been shot directly in the head. The weapon appeared to be a rifle based on a bullet found in the brick wall of the gym. Sergeant Smith suggested the possibility of ex-military involvement.

They still had yet to find the weapon, and this case seemed impossible without much evidence. This office was not set up for solving murders. They had to order information for all the victims from the state database, and the reports had not been received yet. He was trying to keep the Georgia Bureau of Investigation out of it. The GBI had told him that he needed to develop something soon, or they would take over the case.

The Chief knew that the town was struggling with all of this. Everyone wanted answers, and so did he!

He asked his assistant, "Please page Sergeant Smith and Sergeant Nally. "

He wanted to go over everything one more time. While waiting, he looked over the notes they had gathered so far.

The killer appeared to have been in the parking lot, possibly sitting in a vehicle. The ground was a mess from the snow and sleet. There were so many sets of footprints. It was the same with the tire tracks, the tracks had been on top of each other. They weren't even sure where the vehicle had been parked when the shots were fired.

He looked up when there was a knock on the door.

The sergeants entered the room at the Chief's greeting.

"Guess what we just found out! Terry Parker was business partners with Tom Adcock." Sergeant Nally reported.

"What the hell?" The Chief crossed his arms and sat confused. "Why hasn't he called us? He must know, it's been over two weeks."

"I don't know. It's strange that we haven't heard from Tom, since his partner was killed. But it gets worse." Sergeant Smith informed him. "We also received several tips that Tom was at the park that night. No one actually saw Tom but recognized his black SUV. Tom's vehicle is pretty well known around town."

"This is big. We need to get him in for questioning. Surely, he knows something that can help us. Tom Adcock is the connection to the victims and Willowville. Let's get him in!"

Sergeant Nally stood up and gave the Chief the rest of the information. "We ran the reports for Tom and Terry's business. From the reports, P & A Tech seems to be successful. We also ran a report on Tom regarding guns. He owns a few, but not anything that would match the bullet found, and he hasn't purchased any guns recently."

The Chief chuckled, "Well, we all know Tom has guns. Running a gun report was probably unnecessary. I have known Tom and his family for a long time."

"Do you think Tom was meeting the victims at the park?" Sergeant Nally questioned. "Hopefully, Tom will be able to help us piece together some things."

"I will call Tom myself and have him come in," the Chief said.

After the sergeants left, the Chief sat contemplating Tom's possible involvement. He figured Tom would be busy with all the aftermath he must be dealing with. Tom would have to settle company affairs. He put a note on his calendar to call him this afternoon for a meeting. Maybe Tom could help clarify why Terry and his wife had been in town and what they were doing at the park. He assumed that they had been with Tom during their stay, but what they were doing at that park would be crucial.

That afternoon, on the other side of town, unaware of the conversations happening at the police station, Tom was in his home office awaiting information from his company.

His dead partner, Terry, had not said one thing about anything shady going on. They had talked for almost two hours the week prior to the murders about how wonderfully things were going for the business.

They were amazed at how good life had been for them. They were doing jobs they loved and living good lives. The business had been booming, although they still disagreed on the idea of selling the business. Just as he was trying to wrap his head around all of it, his phone rang. It was a phone number that he didn't recognize, but hopefully, it was his team or his attorney.

When he answered, the voice was loud. "Hey Tom, how's it going, buddy?"

The voice was unfamiliar. "This is Tom. May I ask who's calling?"

"Damn Tom, you would think you would recognize my voice since you've been sleeping with my wife."

Tom paused and his head jerked straight up. "Joe?"

The sound of Joe's laughter filled the air.

Tom had no idea how to respond. Was Brooke there with Joe? Had she come clean to Joe about their meetings? Tom had wanted to contact her to see how she was doing, but now, here Joe was on the phone. And from what Brooke had told him, Joe was not a nice guy.

"What do you want, Joe?" Tom lowered his voice, praying the girls didn't walk in.

Joe responded quickly, "The question is, what do you want, Tom? How much is it worth to you, for your family not to find out what you have been up to?"

Tom didn't answer. He would expect to be cussed out, and quite frankly, he would deserve it. He hadn't meant for this affair to happen. He had been so tired of Amy's depression. He deserved to be punished. He didn't know if Brooke had come clean to Joe or how much he knew. Was he really trying to blackmail him? But before Tom could answer, Joe got louder as he told him.

"You have 48 Hours. You better call me back with the amount you decide or else. I would hate for your daughters to look differently at their precious daddy." Silence. Joe had hung up.

Tom was still staring at the phone when it rang again from an unknown number.

Tom answered swiftly, "Look, you son of a bitch."

A deep breath was taken on the other side of the phone, "Tom? This is the Chief. What in the hell is going on with you? Who did you think was calling you?"

Tom apologized. "I am sorry, Chief. I have just had a lot of calls from solicitors this afternoon."

"We need you to come down to the station. As far as I am concerned, you don't need a lawyer right now, heck, probably never. I have faith we can clear this up very quickly. We know that you were business partners with Terry Parker and that you were at the park the night of the murders. Hopefully, you have some information that will help get all of this behind us."

Tom apologized again before hanging up. There was so much going on, and his world seemed to be crumbling. He swore as he stood up. His team was working hard to clear his name, and now he had to talk to the Chief.

Tom was now angry with Terry. None of this was adding up. He knew that because Terry was his partner, he would be questioned. He needed to figure out how much information that he was going to share with the Chief. He called Stan, his attorney, to prepare.

He couldn't say anything about Brooke until he talked to her. Eventually, he would only mention her if he needed her to vouch for his reason for being at the park. He had left before she did, but at least she could account for his time there.

As he walked back into the living room, he needed to explain why he was leaving. He didn't want to cause Amy any more stress. He hadn't mentioned his business problems with Amy. He looked at her with sadness and wished things had been different. He had married her because he loved her so much. He hated that her depression had taken over her life.

Time to fight! He wanted this to be over. He would fight for Amy and his girls. He needed to meet Brooke as soon as possible.

He picked up his phone and texted Brooke: **Can you please meet me tomorrow at the old swimming hole off of HWY 420?**

Brooke immediately texted back, thankfully: **I am so glad to hear from you. I can't do it tomorrow, but I can meet you there on Friday morning. Does 9:00 work for you?**

He answered: **Yes, that works fine. I hope you are ok**.

There were no other text exchanges. Tom prayed that it was really Brooke who was texting and not Joe. Joe had sounded insane when he called, maybe he had Brooke's phone now and was texting. He would have to take that chance on Friday. He also wished he didn't have to wait until then. But that couldn't be helped. The old swimming hole was a place only known to the locals. It had been used as a teenager hangout for fifty years or more.

Later, Tom nervously walked into the police station. The Chief asked with confusion as Tom sat down. "Why didn't you call us since Terry Parker was your business partner? It sucks that we had to find that out from someone else."

"I have been so busy out in Texas trying to get everything handled with the business that I totally forgot about calling you," Tom replied.

The Chief then asked him about being at the park. Tom couldn't believe that he lied and told him that he thought he had to pick up one of his daughters from basketball practice. Once he realized he had the wrong day, he had headed back home. It was true, just not really for that day.

"I guess I got my days mixed up." Tom had said.

"Were the Parkers or Ray Harper staying with you?" The Chief questioned. "Also, is Ray one of your associates?"

"Terry and Julie were not staying with us, and quite frankly, I didn't know they were in town." Tom was truthful about that. "I don't know who Ray Harper is, and I've never heard Terry mention him."

Tom decided not to mention the missing money in his company. He had to figure that out before telling the police. The Chief wanted to know what Terry had been doing in Willowville, since they lived in Texas. Had he been visiting?

He told the Chief, "Again, I have no idea what they were doing here. I didn't know he wasn't in Texas."

He hated so many lies. All of this was stressing him out. Normally, he didn't lie or hide things. He definitely needed to talk to Brooke about it first. Maybe they could go talk to the Chief together. When he figured out this work stuff, things should be easier.

The Chief ended the conversation, "It's fine for you to travel for now, but we might need you to come back in if anything else arises."

Chapter 7

Brooke stood at the kitchen sink that night, cleaning up from dinner. Frankie was working on a school project and running from his bedroom to the kitchen. He would joke with her, ask questions about his project, and then return to his room. She laughed at him as she watched him. Looking outside, she could see the sun starting to set. It was going to be beautiful, like always. The sky was shades of pink and purple. She turned on the coffee pot and made herself some coffee.

She summoned Frankie and pointed out the window at the sky. "Hey, look at that sunset! Would you like to go sit out on the porch with me?"

He shook his head no and said, "Not tonight! I am almost finished with my project, and I want to play video games until bedtime. Do you mind?"

Frankie smiled at her, and she thought that smile of his could light up a room.

"Of course, I don't mind. I guess I'm just not as fun as those games."

He laughed and raced back towards his bedroom.

She poured herself a cup of coffee. On the way out to the porch, she noticed Joe sitting on the couch and looking at his phone. She almost invited him to join her, but decided not to ask. He would either turn her down or accept and spoil the sunset.

It was much colder than she expected. She lit the porch heater. It didn't take her long to warm up between the fire and the coffee. She thought about the text she had received earlier today from Tom. She had been surprised by his text. It had seemed short and to the point. She assumed he was being cautious in case Joe was there.

Although if Joe had seen it, he would have freaked. A meeting at the swimming hole would have caused World War III. She hated having to wait till Friday, but she had already missed too many days from work because of the snow days.

Brooke thought about the past week. It had flown by. Joe had also been acting differently with her.

He had cooked dinner for the family the night before. He had grilled steaks for himself and Frankie, and chicken for her. When she asked him why, he said because he knew she had been so busy, he wanted to help her. Then he looked at her and said mostly because I love you. It had shocked her.

The shock wasn't because he had said he loved her. She knew that Joe believed he loved her in his own messed up way. The shock was him doing something nice and not rubbing it in her face. Dinner had gone great. When they had finished eating, he had even offered to help clean up. She had declined his help, politely with a smile, and thanked him for offering.

Then while she was cleaning up, he had asked her if she minded if he went down to his garage. She was so confused as he had never asked for her permission before, but said she didn't mind. By the time he returned back to the house, she had already showered and gone to sleep.

Tonight, at dinner, he had been quiet but still nicer than his normal self. Brooke would have invited him out on the porch with her, but didn't want to chance his mood changing. As she tried to figure out his sudden change, he surprised her again.

"Mind if I join you?" Joe asked as he stepped out on the porch.

Although he was making her nervous, she nodded yes. "Of course not, Joe."

He came and sat in the swing with her. He put his arm behind her, up on the back of the swing.

"Brooke, I am sorry how things have gotten between us. I know it's been hard on you."

She felt like she had been hit in the head. This hadn't happened since at least before her daddy died, if ever.

"I'm sorry too, Joe," she answered as the guilt of her recent actions filled her.

They spent the next hour sitting in silence. Neither of them seemed to know what to say. Finally, Joe stood up. "I will let Frankie know he needs to shower and get in bed."

"Thank you. I guess it's shower time for me as well." She stood up and followed him towards the door.

"Brooke, go ahead and do your thing. I will lock up and make sure Frankie gets settled."

A little while later, Brooke stood in the hottest shower she could stand for what seemed like forever. When she came out, Joe had turned on soft music.

Her body started shaking, realizing he was being nice in order to get sex. This wasn't his normal mode.

She said nothing as she got ready for bed but knew she could fake sleep or a headache, if needed.

But when she lay down, Joe surprised her again. "Do you mind if I just hold you, honey?"

She didn't answer him right away. She didn't know what was going on with him this week. Any other time her silence would have angered him. Instead, he lay patiently with her and remained silent as well.

Finally, he said, "I just want to hold you, that's all."

She nodded yes. Fear filled her as she thought he was going to get angry and start raising hell any minute, but he didn't. Joe was still holding her when she fell asleep.

The next morning when she woke up, Joe had left a note. He was headed out early to the office. He hoped she had a great day and that he loved her. Brooke couldn't believe what she was reading.

She dressed and yelled for Frankie to hurry up. When she got to the kitchen, Joe had already made her a pot of coffee. She paused before she drank and shook her head, praying he hadn't poisoned it. She called for Frankie, as it was time to go.

She dropped Frankie off at the middle school and immediately called Shirley to tell her about last night with Joe and how he had acted. His sudden change shocked Shirley as well.

"He actually cooked dinner for us, and then last night, he sat on the porch with me."

"Are we talking about Joe, your husband? What is going on with him?"

Brooke admitted it made her feel guilty about what she had been doing lately with Tom. She still cared for Joe and wanted him to be a better man. Brooke wanted him to finally be the husband she deserved and the father that Frankie deserved.

"And you're not going to believe this either. I haven't smelled alcohol on him all week." Brooke informed Shirley.

"Damn! I can't believe that. I can't imagine him going a day without drinking, much less a week!"

They talked about the text from Tom and the meeting scheduled for Friday.

Shirley warned, "Brooke, just be careful with Joe and his charms."

Joe and Tom were on Brooke's mind throughout the whole day. She cared for Tom, but Joe was her husband. Joe was her son's father. She imagined how amazing life could be, if they could be a happy family. She had dreamed of this for so long, but was it possible?

When Brooke arrived home, she was exhausted from her day at work. Frankie and Joe were playing basketball. They both waved and headed over to her car.

Frankie was really excited, "Mom, Dad's taking us out to eat, if you will say yes! He said we all deserve it."

Joe smiled when she looked over at him. It had been a long time since they had gone out somewhere to eat as a family. "I was hoping we could go now and get back in time to porch sit, as you call it."

She agreed but wanted to freshen up a bit. Both guys were waiting on the porch when she finished.

Frankie whistled as Joe said, "You look beautiful."

She thanked him and winked at Frankie. She was on cloud nine. They ate at one of the local restaurants. It had been pleasant. Frankie had so much fun, and she was sure he didn't remember many times like this. He chatted all the way home. She told him if he would get a shower when they got home, he could play on his video games till bedtime. He skipped his way to the shower.

She headed to her bedroom and changed into her comfy clothes and house slippers. From the living room, Joe told her the porch heater was lit and that he would bring her coffee out when it finished brewing.

He came out smiling and joined her on the swing. She took her coffee and watched him closely.

"Would you mind if I play some music?" He asked.

She nodded no. "That's fine, Joe."

He turned on her favorite, old country music. This was not his style, so she appreciated that he remembered it was hers.

After a while, he took her hand, "Care to dance?" he whispered.

She stood up, and he pulled her close to him. She inhaled – he smelled so good. Again, she noticed there was no alcohol odor. He put his face into her neck. He was being gentle. They swayed until the song stopped. Joe kissed her cheek.

She looked at his face. The years of anger had aged him. Unsure of anything that was happening, she smiled at him. She thought it would upset him if she asked him what was going on, so she remained quiet.

He touched her face. "Brooke, I really am sorry that I haven't been a good husband to you. I wish I could take all these years back. I hope you know how much I love you. I am going to be a better husband and father. I have been such a fool."

The words hit her like a brick. They touched her heart. How long had she waited for this moment?

"Joe, I love you too, and I am sorry." She struggled to speak as her emotions peaked.

"After your dad died, I thought I had to be tougher, tough enough for both of us. I handled it all wrong."

He turned the music and porch heater off. He then held out his hand to her.

She took it and followed him inside. They went to their bedroom and just stood kissing. Joe was moving slowly.

He stopped and reminded her that Frankie would still be up.

Joe offered to go get everything locked up and to make sure Frankie got in bed. "I'll take care of everything." He leaned over and kissed her head. And then he walked out of the room.

Brooke showered and thought about the last few days. She felt warm from Joe's words and actions. As she was drying off, he came into the bathroom.

Her face turned red with embarrassment. Joe had said so many mean things about her body over the years. She wrapped the towel around herself quickly. She didn't look at him. She was ashamed knowing what he saw.

He frowned as he realized why. "I'm sorry."

Brooke put her housecoat on and stretched across the bed. Joe lay down beside her. He stroked her arm, then smiled and admitted. "I feel shy tonight. I guess it's been so long."

She agreed with him and nervously laughed as well.

Joe ran his hand under her housecoat and Brooke flinched. His touch burned and she wanted him, in a way she hadn't ever felt. The housecoat slid away from her body and she reached to pull it back up, to remain covered. Joe stopped her and leaned down and kissed her exposed skin.

"Please, let me love you." His words were mumbled as his face was now pressed against her body. She lay back and he rolled over onto her. Brooke was lost in another world.

Then for maybe the first time ever, Joe made love to her. She was still confused by his change, but cautiously appreciative that he had been so gentle and loving.

Brooke now lay awake at three am. She was feeling guilty and ashamed. All of this, and now she had to meet Tom in the morning. She hadn't thought of Tom at all last night. She knew she still loved Joe. She wanted to stay married to Joe and make it work. She had to tell Tom it was over.

She watched Joe as he slept. He looked peaceful. Maybe those murders had opened his eyes to how short this life could be. Brooke knew that she would never be able to tell Joe about her affair with Tom. He would hate her. She would make it up to him. They could start fresh.

As she was watching him, Joe smiled with his eyes still closed. "MMMM what a sight to wake up to."

She laughed at his words, "You can't see anything – your eyes are closed."

He rolled over on top of her. For the second time in a few hours, Joe gently made love to her again. Her body shook with pleasure. He made sure her wants and needs were satisfied.

That next morning, when Joe left the room, she rolled out of bed, smiling from the night. Joe woke Frankie up while she was getting ready. He tried to get her to stay, but Brooke knew she had to go. She told him she would try to leave work early if possible.

"Do you think that Shirley would let Frankie stay over tonight? I could cook dinner again for us. We can start where we left off this morning." He replied as he winked at her.

She agreed to ask Shirley - maybe it would do them good to have some time alone. She left the house quickly, wanting to get this meeting with Tom over with.

After dropping Frankie off at school, she headed over to Shirley's house. She had an hour to kill before she was supposed to meet Tom. Brooke and Shirley couldn't believe Joe's turnaround.

"I know you think I am stupid. Please don't be mad. I ended up making love to Joe, last night. It was AMAZING!" Brooke confessed to Shirley.

"You know I would never be mad, I just want you to be careful! I wish I trusted him, but I am not there, yet."

"It was the first time since I have been with Joe, that he made me feel wanted. And now I feel like a total slut, I hate myself for cheating."

"Clearly, two men in a lifetime, doesn't make you a slut, you goofball!" Shirley laughed.

"Well, I hate it." Brooke admitted. "Also, would you mind if Frankie stays over tonight?"

Shirley assured her, "Of course, it's fine for Frankie to stay over. If you want and need, he can stay all weekend."

Brooke hugged her. "You are the best friend in the whole world, Shirley. I will make it up to you."

Brooke got in her car and tried to ready herself to end things with Tom.

Chapter 8

TOM WAS STILL WAITING to hear back from his personal attorney and his company. It was now Friday morning, and he was meeting Brooke at nine, at the swimming hole.

It had been hell since the day after the murders. He was worried about lying to the Chief, and also about not mentioning Brooke at all. He knew that the affair would make him look even guiltier than he already did. They would see a liar and a cheater, and decide he was guilty.

This whole experience had made Tom realize he wanted his marriage to work and needed to mend his family. Since the morning of the murders, he had wanted nothing more than to hold Amy. He had been a fool to get caught up in the affair. He hoped Brooke would understand, but he needed to end things with her.

Just as he was thinking of Amy, she walked into the room. Even in her weak state of mind, she was still beautiful to him. Her short blonde hair framed her youthful face. He watched as she poured herself some coffee. He thought how distant they had become over the last year. He would do anything to help her get better and for their relationship to be like before.

"Good morning." She spoke softly. "What are your plans for the day?"

One more time, he had to lie to her. He was over all of this. He was going to tell her everything this weekend, even about Brooke.

"Good morning to you, sweetheart. I've got some errands to run this morning, but I should be home after that. We can go pick the girls up together from school and take them to the rec center if you would like?"

The girls would be out of town all weekend for basketball camp. The plan was for them to leave today after school. They would be back on Sunday at six. It would give them a quiet house to talk and be alone together.

Amy hesitated before shaking her head no.

"I will just wait at home."

They agreed he would pick up food on the way home from dropping off the girls. He hugged her and leaned in to kiss her, but she turned her head.

"I love you, Amy. I'll see you later."

At eight-fifteen, he pulled out of his driveway. He wanted to be at the swimming hole when Brooke arrived.

Meanwhile, Brooke had left Shirley's house and was headed to meet Tom.

She texted Joe: **Hey, I just wanted to let you know that Shirley will be grabbing the boys from school. She is going to let Frankie stay for the weekend.**

She saw Tom's parked car when she arrived. This place brought back so many memories. The swimming hole was part of a creek that had pooled up. A large rock hung over the pooled area, and a rope hung down for them to swing out and then drop into the water. It had made a swimming area for the teens throughout the years.

Her phone pinged, and she looked over to read it.

Joe had responded: **That's perfect. I hope you have a great day. I can't wait to see you. I love you.**

She read the text three more times before she got out of her car. She could see that Tom was moving as hesitantly as she was.

They approached each other cautiously. Things had changed between them. Something that had seemed so right just a few weeks ago, now seemed so wrong. Tom finally greeted her with a quick hey. They went and sat on the large rock that hung out over the creek.

Now looking at the rope, Brooke noticed it was frayed and appeared unsafe. Brooke tried to joke, "No swimming today and no swinging ever again."

They both smiled, as it was only about forty degrees- even with a perfect rope, no one would be swimming today. Tom was quiet.

He finally opened up to her. "I am sorry that we haven't been able to talk. So much has happened since I last saw you."

She sat and listened as he started to explain. "Terry Parker, one of the victims, from the park, was my business partner...."

She gasped, "Oh Tom, I am so sorry. I guess I didn't put it together since you had never told me his full name. But you didn't tell me he was in town?"

"I didn't know he was in town that night. Everything just seems unreal. My accounting team was working on getting an audit from an outside source to allow me to buy Terry's half, but then they stopped. They discovered that Terry had already ordered an internal audit, and it showed missing money."

"I don't understand what you mean by missing money."

"Someone has been stealing money from my company and transferred it to an offshore account in my name."

"What? Oh my God!" Brooke stuttered as she spoke now. "Tom, what are you going to do?"

He continued by telling her about the Chief questioning him, "Once they realized I was partners with Terry Parker, I had to go into the station. Plus, there were a few tips called in from some locals that they had seen my SUV at the park."

Her eyebrows raised. Brooke hadn't thought about anyone seeing them. "Did you tell him that I was there with you?"

Tom quickly told her that he had lied to the Chief. "No, I didn't want to throw you under the bus without speaking to you. I ended up telling him that I thought one of the girls had ball practice, but then I remembered when I got there, it was the wrong day. It had seemed sufficient to the Chief. I just need more time."

Brooke was overwhelmed with everything he had going on. Tom could see she was starting to panic that he had lied.

"I was too scared to tell them about us, as it all makes me seem guilty."

His head dropped as he continued to speak. "I am petrified, Brooke- I know I am innocent."

Brooke nodded, "I believe you, Tom, if you say you didn't steal any money, and I know you didn't kill anyone that night. I was there with you!"

"Tom, I was blown away the last night we were together. It was amazing. But I feel terrible that we let it go that far. You mean so much to me, but..."

"I understand, I feel the same way." Tom asked, "Did you tell Joe everything about us, Brooke?"

Brooke was confused. Joe didn't know anything, and as far as she was concerned, she didn't want him ever to find out.

"Joe can never know what we did! Tom, he would never forgive me. I really want to forget it myself." She despised that she had let herself act on her feelings.

"Joe knows, Brooke. He called me, and he's trying to blackmail me. Joe even threatened me that if I didn't get him money, he would tell my family about our affair! I thought that's why you seemed so distant today." Tom spoke sharply.

Brooke started sobbing.

"I wasn't aware that Joe had called you." She wiped her tears on her sleeve. "I was distant today because I feel guilty. Things have been good these past couple of weeks with Joe. I had decided that I wanted to try and fix my marriage."

Brooke paused, as she was trying to make sense of everything she had just heard.

"Joe has been so kind, gentle, and loving lately. I can't believe that I bought into his act, and meanwhile, he was calling and trying to blackmail you. I feel like an idiot."

Tom put his hand on hers, "I have never been as angry as I was at that moment, Brooke. I thought you had confessed. I am so sorry."

"When I saw you at the conference, I just was taken away by you. I never thought we would end up seeing each other afterward." Tom continued.

"Then our conversations gave me such comfort. I care so much for you, Brooke. It's just different. I love Amy, and I am ashamed of myself."

They both agreed that their affair had been a mistake. It was one they both would have to live with forever.

Tom watched Brooke as she sat still crying. "I was going to try and fix my marriage, but now I am so pissed that I don't know what I am going to do. Tom, I only wish you happiness no matter what. If you need me to talk to the Chief, let me know. I will do anything that I can to help you."

"Let me get this business stuff handled. I will call you if I need anything. Thank you for everything. You brought me back to life."

They hugged each other goodbye at her car.

He watched her drive off and he knew she was angry. Brooke had been blown away from hearing about the call from Joe. Tom wondered how Joe would have known about them if Brooke hadn't told him.

In the car, her tears turned to anger as she returned to her house. She drove faster than normal. She wanted to confront Joe. She was ready for this fight. He had played her. This was unforgivable. He was trying to blackmail Tom! This was it. She was through with Joe!

She would figure out a way to care for her mom. She sobbed, thinking about everything. She drove down their long driveway, with tears streaming down her cheeks. She had wanted to believe his words and actions over this last week. All those words of accountability and responsibility. It had felt so good to be in his arms and believing he was finally going to be good to her.

She parked her car, unbuckled, and stormed towards the porch. She didn't see Joe when she entered the front door. Brooke headed to her bedroom, so thankful Frankie wasn't home for the weekend. She was so angry that she wanted to hit Joe. Grabbing an overnight bag from her closet, she started throwing things into the bag, enough to make it several days without needing to come back. She was done with this marriage.

Brooke heard the back door close. She knew Joe would be in the room any minute now. She tried to prepare herself, as she was afraid of him physically hurting her this time. She knew he had never crossed that line but had come close several times. This might be enough to push him over the edge. He had tried to blackmail Tom for money.

He didn't need money. If only, she had left him years ago. She tried to steady herself. Joe stopped at the bedroom door. The smile he was wearing quickly disappeared as he saw the bag on the bed. The room was silent. Joe's eyes were staring at her – she could feel them. She continued to look down towards the floor.

Finally, she lifted her head, and her eyes locked with his. She was still shaking with anger.

"What the hell is going on, Brooke? What are you doing?" Joe's words were soft and drawn out.

Brooke screamed, "I am done with you and this marriage. I am leaving." Her words echoed in the room.

"I don't understand what you are talking about, Brooke?" You could see his mind trying to process what was happening.

Her voice got louder and stronger, "I'm leaving you, Joe. I will stay with my mom and Shirley for the next week. That should give you time to find somewhere else to live. You can have everything else, but I am keeping this house. It's Frankie's home. You need to get out."

Joe was walking closer to her.

"Don't touch me, Joe. I will call the police on you."

Joe jerked at her words, "The police? I haven't done anything wrong, and I have no idea why you are doing this. We just made love hours ago. We were working on fixing us. What is going on?"

"You played me, Joe. How could you? I talked to Tom, and I know you called him. You tried to blackmail him for money?"

He answered slowly, "Honey, I'm sorry. I shouldn't have called him, but I was so angry. I haven't been playing you. I was going to tell you about calling him after dinner the night I cooked for all of us, but I was just too scared. Things were going great, and I didn't want to spoil it. I hoped you wouldn't ever find out. I really am sorry."

His words were so raw. Seeing this side of Joe, she could hear his pain. She had thought today might make him violent, with her calling him out. The opposite was happening. She walked out of the room and headed for the porch. Brooke sat down on the steps.

Joe followed her as he was trying to explain. "Brooke, I messed up. I have taken you for granted all these years. I blame myself that you stepped out on our marriage. I just wanted Tom to feel the same kind of fear that I was feeling. The feeling that I was going to lose my family. I was so scared that I had lost you."

Over the next several hours, they cried together as they discussed the affair. She told him she hadn't planned on any of it happening. She told him about running into Tom at the rally and how things had progressed from there.

Joe and Brooke ended up back inside the house, curled up on the couch together. Joe had taken accountability for his wrongs and had shown her a side of him that she had never seen.

Brooke was mentally exhausted and ended up falling asleep on the couch. When she woke up, she had a blanket covering her. She slowly got up, not sure what time it was.

"Our dinner is ready if you are hungry," he called from the kitchen.

She was starving. As they ate, Joe told her he never wanted to hurt her again. They enjoyed the meal, and even when the conversation turned to the night at the park, Joe remained calm.

"I need to talk to the Chief. I need to let him know that I was there at the park that night and why. Also, Tom was questioned by the Chief, and he lied about why he was there. Tom didn't tell him that he was there with me."

Joe was worried about this affecting Frankie. He suggested, "We need to hold off for now. Let's wait and see what happens. I would like to go visit your mom together in the morning and then go hiking. Does that sound okay to you?"

Later that night, she texted Shirley: **So much to tell you! Thanks for letting Frankie come over. I will call you tomorrow. Love you all.** Shirley sent back a thumbs up with love.

The whole weekend flew by for them. Joe and Brooke were like newlyweds.

As she was getting ready to pick up Frankie, Joe asked about Shirley and the boys cooking out with them for dinner. That sounded good to her. Maybe she could sneak some private time in with Shirley. She texted Shirley as they headed to the grocery store to pick up some extra stuff.

They went in together. Brooke didn't think Joe had ever been to this grocery store with her. On their way out of the store, Brooke froze.

There sitting in a black car a few rows over, was the man she had seen in her mirror at the park. He was even wearing his orange toboggan. He was watching her. She had been so swept up with everything else that she had forgotten to tell Joe or Tom about him. Joe took her arm and helped her to the car.

Her body felt like it was shutting down. Joe had no idea what was happening to her. She was trembling and was unable to speak.

Finally, when she got herself together, she told Joe everything about the man from the park.

By the time they looked back over to the parking space, the man was gone. Joe told her she was probably just seeing things – maybe it was her imagination. He spent the rest of the ride apologizing to her. She had only been at the park that night because of how he had treated her all these years.

Chapter 9

THE WEEKEND DOWNTOWN AT Tom's house was also very emotional, as he was preparing to talk to Amy. He had dropped the girls off for the bus to camp, and had gone to a local diner near his house and picked up Amy's favorite meal. She loved this place because they served old-fashioned style food. They served real mashed potatoes and made homemade biscuits daily. He also stopped and got her favorite bottle of wine.

Amy had always been into cooking and baking. The girls were constantly in the kitchen with her when they were young. She was so patient with them and had been teaching them how to cook.

Tom dreaded tonight. He despised that he was going to hurt her. She already had enough going on, as she had her own problems. When he had dropped the girls off at the park, it had given him chills thinking about the murders. Now he looked around as he drove through downtown. For a Friday night, things seemed quiet.

He ran into a family he knew through the girls at the restaurant. They, along with the locals, were chatting about how bizarre things were right now, since the murders. If they only knew how much more unhinged it was for him. So far, there had not been a news release posted about his connection to the Parkers. He knew it wouldn't be long before word spread about him being partners with one of the victims. He loved his hometown, but it was full of people who loved to gossip.

When he got back to his house, it was already after seven. It had been a long and busy day. He had already texted Amy that he would be home shortly. She had come out on the porch as he was pulling in. She smiled at Tom as he parked his SUV in the driveway.

She was happy to see he had food from the diner. After they ate, he asked her to join him on the back porch. He wanted to talk to her.

"I have to tell you some things, but I know it will be upsetting."

"None of it matters because I love you, Tom."

He insisted it did. Amy had seemed stronger, in that moment. He wasn't sure what was going on, but she seemed calm. In turn, that made him feel worse. He was about to blow her world up.

"Amy, I have made a terrible mistake. I don't even know how to tell you everything. I hate hurting you."

He watched her face, the sadness sitting right in plain view. "There are a lot of things you need to know, and I am terrified to tell you. I am so scared of losing you. When I went to the November Sales Rally, I ran into Brooke Bradley, and we hung out while we were there at the rally."

To his surprise, Amy was shaking her head yes, like she knew.

"I have been meeting with her since we returned home. I can't believe I have to tell you this." Tom's head hung in embarrassment. "I am so disappointed in myself. I messed up Amy. I slept with her. It was a huge mistake. I was just caught up in the moment."

Tom cried as he explained they had been meeting at Mining Mill Park and had met several times. Now, Amy had tears as well.

Amy whispered, "Tom, I know you cheated, but we can make it through that. I love you, and I know that everything I have had going on hasn't helped. I haven't made things easier."

Tom now seemed more shocked. She had apparently suspected what was going on. He didn't question why she thought he was cheating.

He continued, "It's worse, though. There's more. Amy, you know that the Parkers were murdered at the park, but what you didn't know is that I was there the night they were murdered."

Tom noticed that Amy seemed numb. She also wasn't acting surprised by any of what he said.

"The worst part is that my business is now under an investigation." He paused, "Someone has stolen money, and there are accusations of embezzlement. They are investigating me!"

Amy looked at him harshly, "Embezzlement? Did you steal from the company?"

He quickly stopped her, "No, I didn't take any money, but somehow money was moved offshore into an account set up in my name."

Now, Amy was getting upset. She seemed confused.

They continued to talk.

"I had to go into the police station and talk to the Chief. I lied to the Chief about why I had been at the park." Tom admitted.

"I just didn't want to say anything about Brooke, until I talked to her. I also met with Brooke this morning to end things and I told her what was going on with my company. I also let Brooke know about being partners with Terry and that I had talked to the Chief. It didn't seem fair to her to not give her a heads up, since she would be questioned about me."

Amy had sat silently since the mention of embezzlement. He had taken her hand and begged for her forgiveness.

"You have to believe me - I didn't steal any money. I love you, and I am so sorry for hurting you."

"This is a lot! I need some time to process all of this, Tom."

She took off for the bedroom. He felt horrible for his choices. He didn't want Amy to be hurt, and more than that, he didn't want her to leave him.

He waited about an hour and then knocked softly on the bedroom door.

"Can I come in?" Tom asked.

She allowed him to come in. They lay stretched on the bed until they both fell asleep. He was exhausted. The next morning, Amy said very little to him. He asked her if they could talk.

"I have heard enough. I forgive you, Tom, I love you, and we will make it through this. I don't know how, but we will get out of all of this."

Amy then changed the subject. "I hope the girls are enjoying the camp."

"Me too honey, but I wish you wouldn't push me away."

Amy didn't respond.

Tom and Amy spent the afternoon watching a movie.

Tom now sat in his office, printing every email and text message he had received from Terry over the last year. He couldn't find anything indicating that Terry had planned on being in Willowville. He even pulled and printed his calendar from the last year.

He had just seen the Parkers at the Christmas Party a few weeks before their death. Everyone seemed to be doing really well. Amy hadn't attended this party. She claimed she couldn't face getting on a plane.

At the party, he had made his rounds chatting with all the employees there. Terry had been extra generous and bumped up their employees' Christmas bonuses. Julie had chatted and seemed like she was happier than ever. Terry and Julie were normally like oil and water. They would make mean and hurtful snide remarks to each other.

But this past Christmas had been different. They seemed so loving towards each other. He remembered telling Amy about them when he called her from his hotel room later that night. His trip had been short, and he had flown back home the next day.

He tried to think of anything that might help him figure out who had set up the offshore account in his name. He googled Ray Harper, the other victim. He found very little about the man through an internet search, except he was from the metro area, and was about a year younger than Terry and himself. He also owned a small accounting firm.

He wondered what connection he had to the Parkers. Tom even pulled up rosters from the university that he and Terry had attended. As an alumni, he was able to check each years' graduating class. The name wasn't familiar to him at all, but his graduating class had over 300 students that year. Ray Harper had not graduated with them.

He looked at the years before and after his, with no luck. Tom was losing hope of finding a connection between Terry and Ray. He pulled up Terry's calendar, checking for appointments set with Ray.

He finally found one from four years earlier - Terri had lunch scheduled with Ray Harper. He found no mention of what that meeting was about, and he didn't see Ray's name again. Also, over the last few years, Terry had a standing appointment at three o'clock on Fridays, but each meeting was listed with a different person's name. Tom slammed his laptop closed. He felt hopeless. He now had confirmation that Terry knew Ray Harper but had no idea what their relationship was.

He heard Amy stirring in the kitchen and went to join her. He helped her fix some salads for dinner. They ate and sat in silence. Amy cleaned up and went to her office. She stayed in her office for a long time.

Later that night, he felt her climbing into bed. Tom had turned over and pulled her close to him. Her hair smelt like heaven. He missed their closeness. Their love life had been amazing until this last year. He kissed her head, but she stayed still.

This weekend wasn't going as he had hoped. He needed help. Amy said she forgave him, but it didn't sit well with him. He was guilty of cheating and felt terrible for that, but this other stuff was frightening him.

He prayed that the tech team would find something soon. He wanted to know what computer had been used in the crime. He knew that his computer was clear. He was angered at the thought of someone stealing from his business. He had put his heart and soul into the company.

On Sunday, Tom called his parents, David and Sylvia Adcock, and invited them over for lunch. He needed to let them know about the embezzlement accusations.

Once they arrived for lunch, the conversation was about their condolences for the Parkers. They both knew Terry and Julie, well. They both had even attended the Parker's wedding. They hadn't been around them much since, but they had dined together anytime that the Parkers came to town.

"Gosh, what a terrible situation. I knew it would be more complicated since they were here in Willowville. Your mother and I sent flowers. We are also concerned, because we heard that you had been spotted at the park that night."

"Yeah, I went there by accident." Tom lied and it crushed him.

Tom never mentioned Brooke to them.

"I know you are having to travel more with all of this lately. If y'all need us to, we will help with the girls in any way we can."

After lunch, Tom and his father sat out on the back porch. His father expressed concern about Amy, because she hadn't spoken a word during lunch and seemed sad and distant. He and Sylvia had watched her change over the last year as well.

"How is therapy going for Amy?" his father asked.

"It's going about the same. I really am at a loss on how to help her, Dad. When she goes to therapy, Amy twists her hands for the entire hour. The therapist has diagnosed it as depression."

Tom paused as he stared across his backyard, overwhelmed by so many emotions. "And now since the murders, she has become even more distant."

The talk turned to Ray Harper, the other victim. Tom explained he had never met or even heard of him. He told his father that he had tried to research about him.

"I was trying to figure out how Terry knew this Ray Harper, but I haven't been able to find anything." Tom confided to his father.

"Tom, it can't look good that you were at the park on the night of the murders considering your connection to Terry and Julie."

"On top of that, Dad, Terry had ordered an internal audit, without anyone knowing, and money is missing!"

"Money missing? What are you talking about?"

"The audit, and further research, showed money was moved to an offshore account, and Dad, the account was in my name. I want to know WHY Terry ordered the audit to begin with, and now I am scared to death! They are using accusing words like embezzlement!"

Tom sat with his head down. He couldn't look at his father. He wanted to scream.

"Son, you know we love you and support you completely, but if you need to tell me something, please tell me now." David's heart broke as he said it.

Tom yelled and couldn't believe what he had just heard.

"Dad, I didn't kill them! Is that what you mean? Do you believe I would steal from my own company? I haven't stolen anything since I was five and took candy from the gas station, and you guys made me go back in and return it. I will never forget the embarrassment I felt that day. I definitely didn't kill anyone. I haven't been hunting since I was a teenager. I didn't even like the idea of shooting a deer."

Tom's words cracked. His father was crying now, as he hated that he had hurt Tom more with his words.

"I am sorry! Of course, we don't believe you would do either of those things. We just had to clarify. We want you to know if this goes further, we will help you financially all we can. Your mom and I have put a lot into savings all these years. We both wanted to secure your future if we died." He smiled as he said, "We won't be taking it with us."

By the time Tom's parents left, he felt worse than ever. If his own parents thought there might be a chance he had stolen money or killed someone, what would other people think?

Amy had gone into her office and told Tom to let her know when he was headed to get the girls. His girls, what would they think? Tom was running out of time, and he was stuck. He couldn't fix anything until the tech team figured out whose computer was used to set up the account and moved the money. His attorney had yet to give him any new information. His life was in limbo. His marriage seemed to be in limbo now as well.

Chapter 10

THE FOLLOWING WEEK, FOUR men sat around the conference table at the P & A Tech headquarters in Texas. Tom sent his personal attorney, Stan, in his place as the attorney had suggested he not attend. The others included Steve, John, and the tech team manager.

John primarily led the meeting. He had many concerns, as they all did. Each of these men had known Tom a very long time. They each had personally worked with Tom for years. This was a difficult meeting.

"I know that each of us has a great personal and working relationship with Tom, but today we must put that aside. We must look at the facts and make our decisions solely from those facts."

Tom's attorney, Stan, stood up, walked around the table and interrupted John.

"I disagree. I shouldn't have to remind you, but we do have to consider Tom's loyalty to this company. He has proven time after time how much he cares for this business. Tom has never given any of you a reason to distrust him."

"I understand your frustration. I think a lot of Tom, as well. I have reviewed the reports regarding the funds trail over and over." Steve advised them. "Yes, the transfers were done carelessly, but the facts remain where the money landed. The withdrawals had been spread apart over several months and were all under the "Red Flag" amount, an amount that will sound off cyber alarms. Then, the money was transferred straight to the offshore account in Tom's name."

"Yeah, but would Tom have really used his own name if he was stealing money?" John offered.

Stan blurted out, "And he could have just sold the company last year based on the offer, if he wanted or needed the money!"

"Unless he was trying to see if he could get away with it. Some people like the idea of committing a crime just to see if they can." Steve responded.

John reminded Stan that they all wanted Tom to be innocent. John looked down and scribbled the words, "Evidence is too obvious".

Stan apologized and said, "I just think this is all a waste of time. I think your team needs to use their skills to trace down the computer used for the transfers."

Steve nodded. "I agree. Also, you need to be aware that the Willowville Police Chief has contacted me. They were following up since Tom has connections to this murder investigation. As I am not Tom's personal attorney, I don't know how long I can hold off speaking to the Chief. I have made myself unavailable for each contact from the police so far."

The tech team manager spoke up, "It could take a month or so to trace down the information for us to find the computer that was used for the crime. If everyone can stall involving the law, I will prioritize this for the whole team."

Steve had previously dealt with many embezzlement cases, but this one didn't sit well with him. He really was hoping they could get Tom's name cleared.

The meeting was cut short as no one believed that Tom was guilty of anything. They did not get around to talking about Tom's rejection to the idea of selling the company. They each headed out of the office eager to resolve this, except John, who stayed sitting at the table.

John remembered the first time he met Tom and Terry. They both had been so eager when they were setting up the company. He didn't think that Tom or even Terry had the ability to pull such a scam. And now Terry was dead. Someone had killed him and his wife. After all these years with the company, he couldn't believe this was happening.

John scratched his beard as he started looking through prior emails and meeting notes. He noticed a little over a year ago, notes from a meeting where Tom had become very upset with Terry surrounding the company's proposed offer to sell. He remembered how angrily Tom had told Terry-over his dead body would they sell this company. To John, that had seemed like very extreme behavior.

The assistant had not recorded Tom's strong words, the meeting notes had only stated that Tom was angry and unwilling to budge on the proposal to sell the company. He also remembered meeting with Tom afterward, and he was still furious. Tom repeated multiple times that he didn't want to sell the company. He wanted to stay in the business for about five or ten more years. Additionally, he loved the employees and didn't want to see any of them lose their jobs.

It didn't make sense that Tom would be dumb enough to move money into an account in his name. John also wanted to know what Terry was doing in Willowville and why he had requested the audit privately. Had he suspected Tom of stealing? The story just didn't add up.

John had a great relationship with Tom and Terry. He needed to talk to Steve privately. Maybe they needed to speak to the Chief to let him know what was happening in Texas.

John phoned Steve and invited him to meet for lunch. When they sat down at the restaurant just down the road, John brought up the meeting notes from last year and how angry Tom had been. Steve said he remembered that meeting. He had never seen Tom so upset.

Both remembered that Terry had appeared to be sincere about wanting to sell. When Tom had brought up the employees that would lose their jobs, Terry had offered solutions to that as well. Tom had shut him down. John and Steve were at a loss.

Tom was a good man and had seemed like an outstanding person these last fourteen years. John and Steve agreed they had enjoyed working for both of them. Julie, Terry's wife, had also been a great asset to the company as well. The few times they had seen Tom's wife, Amy, they liked her, and she was always friendly and kind to them.

"My gut says that Tom is not involved in this as it appears, but after thinking back to how angry he was over the chance to sell, it changes how I see it a bit." John admitted. "Do you think Terry's murder has something to do with the missing money?

"Maybe? I don't know, but I think we owe it to Terry, to allow justice to be served. Hopefully that will clear Tom's name and allow Terry's murder to be solved."

By the end of the lunch, they both agreed they couldn't wait a month. No matter what they thought of Tom, Terry deserved a full investigation. They each left with heavy hearts.

Steve returned to his office and made the call to the police Chief in Willowville. Thomas Adcock was now part of an embezzlement investigation.

"Hello, this is Steve Jennings, the attorney for P & A Tech in Texas. I am sorry that I have been unavailable, but I was returning your call." Steve said.

"Mr. Jennings, thank you for calling. I wanted to get some information about how things had been between Tom and

Terry at the office. We just want to take a deeper look at their relationship."

"Well, I hate to tell you this, but as of today Tom is under an internal investigation by the company for embezzlement. At the moment, all we know is money is missing, and the offshore account is in Tom's name." Steve paused as he heard the Chief inhale loudly.

"Damn!" The Chief cursed, "I'm sorry. This is just hard to hear because I care about Tom and his family."

"I know, me too. We feel that Tom has been loyal to this company since it started. I know Tom very well, and I don't want to believe he stole money from his own company. It is out of character for him, but with money, it sometimes changes good people.

The Chief advised him that Tom had a lot going against him lately with the case. He had been as shocked as they all were about the embezzlement charges.

"Chief, I will keep you up to date with any new findings." Steve said as he sat with his arms crossed and his mind racing with thoughts and guilt for sharing this information against Tom.

When the call ended, he called John and let him know that he had spoken to the Police Chief in Georgia.

Chapter 11

ALMOST TWO MONTHS AFTER the night of the murders, Tom sat at his desk in his home office. Amy was in the other room. Everything had continued to fall apart since the weekend after seeing Brooke, when he had come clean to Amy.

Amy had spent most of that weekend avoiding him. She still was shutting him out and not talking about any of it. He wondered now why she told him she thought he had been seeing someone. He wasn't sure why she suspected it though because he had never done anything like that before. He wished that she would yell and cuss, just a reaction of any kind would be encouraging.

She seemed distracted. She told him she would forgive him because she loved him. He prayed she meant it. She was still keeping her distance since that weekend. He couldn't tell if she was angry at him or if it was just more sadness from her depression. He wanted her to be better. He needed her support right now, more than ever.

The tech team had informed Tom that they were still working on tracing the money transfers and trying to find the computer used for those transactions.

When Tom was informed that John and Steve had been in contact with the Police Chief, he became even more terrified. The Chief had contacted him last week and let him know that he now had to remain in town until he informed him otherwise. He was no longer allowed to leave the area until this was cleared up.

His life was out of control. Tom hadn't heard anything from Brooke, and he worried that she was in her own mess. The last time that he saw her, he knew she was confronting Joe about the blackmail. The only good that had come from the blackmail conversation was that Joe hadn't contacted him again.

His parents were keeping up with everything going on, as well as helping with the girls and their schedules.

The girls would be devastated, his heart hurt as he thought of them. They assumed that his parents had been helping because of Amy. For now, he wanted to keep the girls from knowing anything more. Although, word had spread through town that he was partners with one of the victims.

On the other side of the wall, Amy sat looking at her computer. She was so ashamed - this was all her fault. Normally, she would have gone to Tom, and he could have helped her. She loved him so much. But now, he would hate her for what she had done.

She thought of all the crime stories she had studied over the last year, and none of them prepared her for what to do. They had all been about normal people that just made stupid choices. She had made foolish choices. Amy couldn't figure out a way to fix this. The police were after Tom, and his office was after him too. She wished now she had talked to Tom all those months ago.

Chapter 12

BROOKE THOUGHT ABOUT THE last couple of months as she got ready for work. She was singing. It had been two months since the horrible night at Mining Mill Park.

She and Joe were still like newlyweds. He was treating her like an equal and loving on her, and she was eating it up. It was what she thought a normal marriage should be. Joe went grocery shopping with her almost every time she went. They took turns cooking meals and sometimes cooked together. Joe was spending a lot of time with her and Frankie. She was really enjoying it.

They had talked more about the night of the murders. Joe wanted her to not get involved with the investigation. He didn't see a reason since she couldn't offer them anything more with the investigation. Joe said his biggest concern was putting Frankie through all of it. Brooke's affair would come out locally, and Frankie would hear about it in school.

This town was small, and talk would spread quickly. Brooke had agreed with Joe, for now. She didn't see a reason to get involved at this point. She hadn't heard from Tom again, so she assumed he didn't need her to vouch for him. She also hadn't seen the man in her mirror again, and she suspected Joe was right and maybe her mind had been playing tricks with her.

Joe came in and pulled her close to him.

"You smell nice!" He said as he planted kisses on her neck.

She put her arms around him. "Joe, you have blown me away! I forgot how much I needed you."

"I have to work in the office today but shouldn't be too late getting in." He said as he continued to smile at her.

"That's fine, Joe. I will pick Frankie up and visit my mom tonight without you."

He continued to kiss her, but she slowly pushed him away.

"Not this morning, sweetheart - we both have a lot to do." She wanted him to trust her again.

Joe had taken all the blame and wouldn't let her apologize for anything. Her heart still felt guilty, though. Tom had only crossed her mind a few times since their meeting.

As she looked up, Joe was still watching her. "Don't be hard on yourself. All that matters is I love you, and you love me."

She knew he was right. She wanted to think she had forgiven Joe for his past behavior. She wanted to believe he had forgiven her.

Joe drove down the driveway in his big truck. She stood watching him leave with her coffee in hand. She hadn't been alone on the porch in a long time. Joe always joined her now.

Shirley pulled in only a short time after Joe left. She walked up to the porch with Reece following behind her. The boys then quickly took off in the yard running.

Today was a teacher's workday, so the boys were out of school. Frankie was going to spend the day at Shirley's. Shirley had taken a few days off to work on some things at her house.

"You should play hooky with me today! It would be fun for us and the boys!"

Brooke shook her head, "Not today, Shirley. I have a meeting with an important customer."

By the time Shirley and the boys left, Brooke had to hurry. She needed to be at her meeting in about an hour, and it was a forty-five minute drive. She ran back inside and grabbed her stuff.

She didn't like driving fast anymore. When she was young, she got many speeding tickets, but age and her son had slowed her down. All those years of fear, worrying if something had happened to her, Joe would be raising Frankie.

Later that day, as Brooke was driving home, she stayed in the slow lane. She hated the interstate. It made her nervous when those big trucks waited until they were right on you before jerking over to the next lane to pass you. The day had gone great for her. She had succeeded in closing a big deal. It would mean a huge commission.

The money was great, and she loved closing a sale. The job was hard, but she couldn't imagine not doing this. Brooke had taken her commissions all these years and put them into a savings account in Shirley's name, just as a backup since her marriage had been so strained for so many years.

Brooke was hoping to get Frankie straight from Shirley's so she could go visit her mom. Her mom was still doing well with the new therapy. Seeing her mom taking a turn for the better felt so good. Joe had been going with her most of the time now, and he always made her mom laugh.

She should be at the Willowville exit in about ten minutes if traffic continued moving like it was. Shirley lived out in the country about 15 minutes further out from Brooke. They both loved the privacy and living in the woods but complained about being so far from anywhere. Once she got off the interstate, she turned onto the back road that would take her to Shirley's house.

Down the road, she looked in her rearview mirror and noticed a car behind her that looked familiar. It was the one from the grocery store, the same one that she had seen when she was there with Joe. She tried to calm herself. She couldn't be imagining this – there behind her was the man from the park. He was even wearing the orange toboggan.

She hit the accelerator, but he sped up as well. She looked down and saw she was now doing sixty-five in a thirty-five. She also stupidly realized that her gas light was on again. She only had six miles to empty. She would never reach Shirley's house with the gas tank that low. She turned down another road, and he turned as well. She racked her mind trying to figure out a way back to town without stopping. She was sweating. He was following her.

Brooke jerked the car as she turned on the next road, almost sliding into the ditch. The car behind her slammed on the brakes, then backed up and turned behind her.

Brooke quickly straightened her car and started speeding again. The car behind her accelerated closer to her. She needed to get her bearing because she was now down to four miles to empty. She tried to figure out exactly where she was and where the closest gas station would be.

Suddenly she remembered that the road coming up on the left would get her back to a gas station. She tried to calm herself, but she could barely breathe. She told herself if she could get there, she should be safe since it was a public place. She could lock herself in the car until she could call Joe. The car slid again as she made the turn, but the other car still followed behind her. She cursed herself for forgetting to stop for gas again.

As she approached the store, she turned her blinker on and turned into the Green gas station. She looked back and saw that the car did not stop, but he watched her as he slowly drove by. She was shaking. She picked up her phone and called Joe.

"Just stay in the car, and I am on my way. I should be there within forty-five minutes or less."

When he pulled up, Brooke was sitting in her car, still shaking.

He leaned down and helped her stand as he hugged and held her.

"It's okay sweetheart. Go get in my car and wait. I will be right back."

Joe moved Brooke's car to the pumps and filled up her tank. He then parked her car off to the side of the store and went back to his car. She was crying.

"I was so scared. I almost wrecked so many times! I was going so fast, and I was scared he would kill me, Joe. It was the man from my rearview mirror, from the park. I was just trying to get away from him!"

"Honey, you never have to worry about any of this again. I promise you that. I will ensure you always have a full gas tank from now on."

He held her close to him. He warned her that he thought she should take some time off from work.

"This situation is too much for you. Your imagination seems to be going wild. I prefer you not be out alone. Let's go get Frankie and go to your mom's house. We can return to town for dinner and pick up your car afterward. That way, I can follow you home."

"Joe, that's too much trouble for you," she started to say, but he cut her off. He wasn't having it any other way.

When they arrived, Shirley immediately thought something horrible had happened to Brooke's mom. Brooke looked as if she had seen a ghost, and Shirley wasn't expecting Joe to be there with her.

"Oh god! What's happened?"

"On my way here, the man from the park chased me in his car. Then because I am an idiot, I was about to run out of gas again. Thank God, I was able to make it to the gas station. It was horrible."

"Holy crap! I am so grateful Joe was able to race like he did to you!"

Shirley surprised them all by reaching over and hugging Joe. She then asked, "Did you guys call the law?"

"No, not yet. I'm going to try and dig up some information on the car Brooke described." Joe said. "I feel like Brooke needs some time off, don't you, Shirley?"

Shirley smiled, as she liked that idea. She knew that would give her friend time to heal and be safe. Also, it would allow them to hang out more.

"Why don't you and Reece join us for dinner?" Joe invited Shirley and her son. "We can all fit in the truck and ride together?"

"That would be great, but our supper is on the table already. Maybe next time."

As Shirley watched them leave, she was still worried for Brooke and still questioning Joe's sudden change. He sure seemed like he was sincere. She prayed for her friend's sake that it was real. She loved seeing Brooke so happy.

Shirley still worried about this man whom Brooke thought had followed her. Could he be the killer? Joe said she probably was just seeing someone that looked like the same guy, and was just headed in the same direction. That could be true, Brooke had a big imagination. Maybe she was just getting confused, reading into something that wasn't there.

They decided to skip her mom's house as Frankie was starving to death, according to him. Frankie wanted barbeque, so they drove to the next town over. Brooke was starting to calm down, but only because she didn't want to worry Frankie.

She had been grateful to Joe, for handling things like he did. He smiled at her as she sat down across from him. She smiled back. Everything was going to be okay. They chatted about her work meeting and the closing of such a big deal. Frankie talked about his day with Reece.

"Mom deserved a steak tonight to celebrate her big sale, didn't she Frankie?"

"Well, this is like a steak, right Mom?"

She laughed and she told him that eating with her boys was the best celebration no matter what they ate.

After dinner, they headed to the Green gas station. Frankie had fallen asleep in the back seat of Joe's truck, and she didn't want to wake him. She assured Joe she would be fine with him driving behind her. "Thank you again, Joe."

Joe had to keep his patience intact. Brooke drove like an old lady. If the sign said thirty-five, she went thirty-five. Following her gave him time to think, though. Joe was concerned with "mirror man" as Brooke called him. Why was he following her?

Finally, they were pulling into the driveway. Joe reminded himself, this is how you show someone you love them. He needed to control his feelings.

Chapter 13

ERIC STINSON WALKED OUT on his porch and lit up a cigarette. He had visited with his mom today. He had taken some time off from work. His mother had been worried sick about him ever since the night at the park. The sight of Julie Parker's face flashed through his mind. One exit bullet hole on her forehead, the size of a silver dollar, maybe bigger.

When he rolled her over, he already knew she was dead. He also had learned from his buddies at the police station that the bullet used on Julie was found on the front of the gym lodged into a brick.

Eric knew a lot about guns. He owned quite a collection of them. He had been hunting with his father and grandfather since he was nine years old. They had taught him to shoot a gun even earlier than that.

Eric had talked to Tom many times over the last several months. Tom had told him how bad things were going with his business and had also shared that they were looking at him for embezzlement.

He never mentioned to Tom that he knew that he had been at the park that night. He also didn't tell him that he knew he was there with Brooke. Eric had been furious with Tom, but didn't want to discuss it.

Eric loved Tom like a younger brother. His real brother had died when Eric was ten years old. His brother had only been eight years old. His brother had fallen off a boat and drowned. His family had been devastated. Eric could remember the day like it was yesterday.

He thought of Tom's wife, Amy, and their daughters. He was very fond of Amy. The girls looked just like Amy had at their age. Eric thought about when they were young. He was two years older than Amy and Tom and four years older than Brooke and Shirley. He remembered when Brooke started driving, they all would gather out at the old swimming hole on Hwy 420.

They spent a lot of time together out there. A group of about twenty people would hang out. Since that first summer, he hung out with them, he had been in love with Shirley. He followed them around like a puppy. He wanted to wait until Shirley was eighteen before he asked her out though to be respectful since he was older. He planned on asking her after she graduated, but that summer she had taken care of her dying father and he never had the chance. Those two months had flown by, and then she had taken off for college.

A few years later, Eric had met Cindy. She had swept him away. She was a city girl, who had been hired as a consultant for the county to help organize the Recreation Department.

Eric smiled, thinking back at how different he and Cindy had been, but how well they had gotten along. They married soon after they started dating, right after his twenty-fifth birthday. Their marriage was perfect until that horrible day.

Cindy was killed in a car wreck one week before he turned twenty-nine. Eric spent years grieving over her. He told his mom then that he never wanted to love again.

His life had been filled with one tragedy after another. From his brother's death, his grandfather's death after his high school graduation, Cindy's death, and eventually his father about five years ago. Cancer had taken his father, but he blamed himself. He felt responsible. His father had been on hospice, and it was his night to stay over so that his mom could rest. One hour after she went to bed, his father took his last breath.

Eric sat now on his porch swing, chain-smoking. He was thinking of all the tragedies that had surrounded him over the years. He again thought about Julie Parker's dead body lying on the ground.

Trying to erase the image, he remembered a time when he wanted a whole house full of kids, but he would never have that. They had tried throughout their whole marriage to get pregnant, but were unable. He assumed it just wasn't in the cards for him.

He had been satisfied working with all the kids, all these years through his job at the recreation center. Until these last several months, that had changed. He was watching two people he loved, that were blessed with families, throwing it away.

He hadn't told the Chief that he recognized Julie as the dead lady, and he definitely hadn't told him about Tom's meetings with Brooke at the park. He remembered the last trip he had taken with Tom out to Texas, he had been angry with Tom. On that trip, Tom had told him that he was thinking about divorce because he didn't recognize Amy anymore, as she was so withdrawn. Tom had a wife and family to love, and he was giving up on them.

When his mom had brought up the rumors about Brooke's husband being a snake, he felt sorry for her. But he had no sympathy for Tom. He knew Amy was good to him. Yeah, this last year, things had been harder, but she deserved better from him. When he spoke to Tom now, he needed to be cautious – if only Tom knew how angry he had become. He picked his phone up and pulled up Brooke's name.

On the other side of town, Brooke sat waiting at the bus stop for her son Frankie. Her phone rang. She didn't recognize the number but grabbed it quickly thinking it might be a customer.

"Hello, this is Brooke." The phone was silent on the other end. "Hello?"

The call disconnected. Brooke studied the number. She hit send and called back. The call went to voicemail immediately, followed by an automated message that the voicemail you are calling is full. So, she hung up.

Brooke looked up as she heard the school bus stopping. The lights were flashing as the stop sign flag went out. Frankie came bouncing down the steps and over to the car. He hopped in, and they started chatting about his day.

Brooke's phone pinged: **Brooke, I am sorry that I hung up. Can we talk?** She nervously put the phone back in her lap, it would have to wait.

She and Frankie were heading to get his haircut. As Frankie chatted, she tried to concentrate on him and on driving.

Frankie was telling her that he loved her more than anything and would do anything for her. It caught her by surprise, the way he was talking.

She laughed and asked him, "Is there something bothering you, sweetheart? That's a pretty big statement."

"No," he said quickly. "I just wanted you to know."

She smiled over at him. She told him she loved him so much and she would do anything for him. She was on edge about everything these days.

As she said it, her phone pinged again. **Brooke, it's really important**.

Brooke thought, who was this? Could this be from Mirror Man? She deleted the message and the number from her phone.

Chapter 14

THE MARCH WINDS WERE blowing hard today. Larry looked to the side mirror of his motorcycle at the road stretched behind him. Willowville had so many great routes for bike riding.

He lived on the edge when it came to riding his motorcycle. He often went too fast as he loved the thrill. Larry had taken a liking to the curvy roads here that went on forever.

It helped that the sights around the area were breathtaking. Trees were all around, and the mountains lined the sky. He should bring his wife up here soon. But today, he had business to take care of. Larry sped around the curves with the bike almost lying over. He had over an hour until his meeting.

He loved his job, but sometimes you worked with people that turned out to be bad people. He was riding to clear his mind. He wasn't looking forward to the meeting today. He thought riding with so much free time on his hands would be nice before the meeting. He normally had to drive his car when he was working, so this was a nice change.

He noticed a beautiful farmhouse sitting in a field at the bottom of the mountain. Fences lined the property, and the area was full of cows. It was a beautiful sight with a creek flowing right beside it. He pulled over to take a picture for his wife.

She would love this area. Larry removed his helmet and started snapping pictures of the farmhouse and mountains ahead of him.

Maybe they could move to a small town like this when he retired. His wife always talked about their retirement. Larry was almost ready for retirement. She told him stories of how they could spend their time. She wanted a Honeybee Farm and talked about going to craft fairs to sell their honey for extra income.

The pictures he took were amazing. He looked at his phone to see the time and knew he still had a while to go. There was no traffic today. He thought about work, and he had enjoyed his job until a few months ago. He couldn't forget the night in January, and it was causing him to lose sleep. He hated what had happened.

Larry pulled his orange toboggan down around his ears, as it was cold today with the strong winds. It had been colder that night in January, it had snowed, and by the time he got back to his house, it was just raining. Funny how snow was on the ground in one area, and an hour away, it was just a cold rain.

He hopped back on the bike - time to take advantage of this sunshine and clear roads.

Larry hadn't passed a car in miles when he noticed a vehicle fast approaching him from behind. He saw the curve signs as he tried to keep an eye on the car behind him. He wasn't sure if the car could see him.

When the car was close enough, he knew the driver saw him. He had no time to think, as the car was starting to pass him. They were in the curve, and this idiot didn't care.

When he looked over, he saw a familiar face. The car swerved back into his lane of the road, and before he could correct the bike, his tires caught the shoulder of the road. It jerked him totally off the road. The rear end hit something, maybe a rock. The bike, and Larry, went flying off over the embankment. The drop was over thirty feet.

The motorcycle immediately exploded when it hit the bottom. Flames could be seen from the road. About ten minutes later, a car passed by on their way home and saw the fire. They called 911 as the fire was spreading.

Once the fire trucks and police arrived on the scene, they raced into action. It wasn't long after they got the fire out, that they realized it had been started from a motorcycle crash. The tag had been jarred off at the top of the road.

Hours later, the case was closed. The tag had made the police officers' jobs easier as they were able to identify the registered owner. Larry Jones, of the metropolitan area, was now dead.

Two local Metro police officers informed Larry's wife that evening of his crash. She was devastated. Larry had told her he was taking the day off to ride his bike. Now he was gone.

That night, someone sat looking at their social media accounts for information about a specific event. By 10:30, reports showed up about Larry Jones and a deadly motorcycle crash on HWY 420. The person sat smiling at the thought of seeing the motorcycle and Larry soar off the road. The explosion had been exhilarating, and the display had looked like fireworks!

Chapter 15

THE CHIEF SAT AT his desk - he felt ashamed. It had been over two months now since the night of the murders. They really had nothing more now than they did when the murders took place. Tom Adcock was the only suspect but was just listed as a person of interest at this point.

He didn't believe that Tom could have killed three people. He did wish Tom had been upfront about the embezzlement investigation. The P & A Tech attorney had clarified that no charges had been formally filed yet.

They all wanted answers. If Tom was the killer, then it would explain the embezzlement and vice versa. The Chief and his team had spoken to a handful of people from the business since then, but no further information had been obtained.

The Chief thought about Tom and why had he really been at the park. Tom admitted he was there, but claimed he didn't know why the Parkers were there. Had his partner come there to confront him about embezzling and Tom shot them?

The Chief and his community were demanding answers. Sergeant Nally knocked on his door.

"Hey Chief, I've got more bad news, sir. "

The Chief sat quietly and motioned him in, awaiting this new news.

"A 9-1-1 call was made from Tom's house the night of the murders. Amy Adcock had called around nine-forty and was reporting her husband wasn't home and that she was afraid someone was there in the house. During the call, she then advised the operator that her husband had just pulled up in the driveway. The operator didn't send anyone out as she thought that since he was home, it didn't matter."

"So, Tom wasn't home like he had said?" The chief questioned.

They all agreed that they needed to bring Tom's wife, Amy, in for questioning.

The Chief sat thinking. Tom had lied about being at home after mistakenly going to the park to pick up one of his daughters. The Chief shook his head. He was so disappointed to think that Tom had lied to him and had not mentioned the embezzlement charges.

The Chief told the Sergeant that he would make the call to Amy. He knew from Tom's parents that she was fragile.

He wasn't sure how to handle this, but he knew he had to talk to her to determine exactly what time Tom had arrived home. Otherwise, Tom was now a suspect, not just a person of interest.

He called Tom's Dad, David, out of courtesy, from his personal cell phone to keep it off the record.

"Hey, David?" The Chief replied when he heard David's hello. "This is the Chief." There was a moment of silence that followed.

"Chief, how's it going?"

"I really hate to bother you. We need to bring Amy in for questioning."

David sighed, "Why?"

"I really can't tell you anything more at this time. I am calling you off the record. I just wanted to make sure the girls would not be there when I called her."

"Tom is not guilty! What the hell are you questioning Amy for?" David Adcock was angry.

"I get it. Man, I wish I didn't have to do any of this. But I don't have a choice, we have to ask her some questions." The Chief did understand David's anger.

"Can you give me about an hour? I will get things arranged."

"Yes. Also, please don't tell Amy why you are getting the girls because I am going off protocol trying to help you guys out."

David was still upset, and his words conveyed the tension. "It doesn't feel like you are trying to help, or you guys would be out finding the real killer!"

When an hour had passed, the Chief picked up the desk phone and dialed Amy Adcock's house. Surprisingly, they still had a home number.

Amy answered the phone slowly. She rarely got calls on this phone. Usually, if someone dialed it, they wanted to sell her something. As soon as the caller stated his name, Amy wished she hadn't answered.

"Amy, this is The Chief."

Amy inhaled loudly when he announced himself.

"It's ok, there is nothing to worry about, but we need to ask you some questions. I can come there, if you would like?" He offered.

"No, the girls just left with David. I can come to the station."

Amy was starting to freak out, but kept her emotions at bay, so the Chief would not suspect anything.

"How much time do I have before I need to come in?" she asked cautiously.

"Within the next hour, please." The Chief replied.

She thought she couldn't move out of town in an hour. She had been caught. She still wasn't ready to tell Tom.

Amy scrambled around the room. She didn't know what to do. She had an hour to figure this out.

She waited another thirty minutes and called the police station back. She asked to speak to the Chief.

"Is there any way we could put this off until tomorrow?"

"We really need you to come on in now." The Chief shook his head as he hung up the phone.

Meanwhile, Amy was calling her father-in-law. She told him she had to go to the police station and didn't want to upset Tom about it. She asked that he please not say anything. Tom's dad had agreed and told her to call if she found out anything.

David offered to have the girls stay there with them for the night. She loved Tom's family. They had been so good to her and the girls. Her head hung in shame as she considered how much this would disappoint them all.

Amy gathered herself and headed to the station. She was running out of time. How much could she tell the Chief? If only Julie hadn't reached out to her over a year ago. Julie had pretended to be her friend. She said she cared about all of them and only wanted what was best for Tom and Terry.

Now Terry and Julie were dead. Tom was a suspect. Tom had been cheating on her. He had told her his version of the story, but now thinking about it, she hated that he had lied to her about not knowing about the embezzlement before the murders.

She had known about the affair since the first night that Tom had met Brooke at the park. Tom told her that he had lied to the Chief about why he had been at the park. She knew he was there with Brooke. She knew because she had seen him - she was there too. She had used the location tracker on her phone, and she knew every move he made.

Tom was a fool, Amy thought. The police could access any details of anyone's life if they needed through someone's phone. He should have known that they would have been able to track him.

She could have solved this case on the night of the murders. She smiled a little at the thought of how educated she had become on case-solving now. So much had happened this past year or so. She had hidden in her house for almost the entire year. The more she researched, the more aware she became of the criminal mind.

Amy arrived, and kept her head down in the waiting area while waiting for the Chief. This room was full of criminals that would now see her face. She was afraid these criminals would now know her. They could come after her. It was easy to find people if you had a picture of their face. The internet had changed the game for criminals. No one was safe. She jumped when her name was called.

Keeping her head down, she walked to the Chief's office. They closed the door behind her. The Chief and two sergeants were in the room. The Chief said that they only had a couple of questions for now, and they would be quick.

He apologized that Amy was in this position. They informed her that she had the right to an attorney to be present if she wanted one. Amy knew she had that right. She came alone because for now she needed more time. She would take the chance. They were only questioning her about Tom, she reminded herself. They didn't know anything about her.

She declined an attorney and told the Chief, "It's fine, and I understand my rights."

"Amy, Tom stated that he left the park and came straight home. Can you please confirm what time Tom came home on the evening of January 8, the night of the murders?"

Amy knew the importance of this question. "Tom did not come into our house until around 9:45 pm."

She remained quiet after answering him.

"Thank you for letting us know that. Did you know the Parkers would be there at the park that night?"

Now the Chief was trying to trick her, and she was not going to fall for it.

"Yes."

The Chief told her that was all they needed for now. She asked the Chief to please keep their conversation private.

"I didn't tell Tom that I was coming here." The Chief looked confused at her. He felt like she knew more than what had been asked but for now, he needed to figure things out before he went further.

On Amy's way back home, she was relieved. The Chief had only asked her those two questions. She hadn't lied. She knew that either of those questions could be easily checked. Tom's phone would show the time he left the park, and her phone would show that the Parkers would be in Willowville that night.

Her biggest mistake was calling 9-1-1 after she tried to call Tom and he didn't answer. She had thought someone was at their house and Tom wasn't back yet. She had been afraid and hid in the closet until she heard his vehicle. By then she was already on the call with the emergency operator.

Chapter 16

Normally, Brooke kept away from the news, but two weeks ago reports had spread of more tragedy in Willowville. They were all talking about the crash on Hwy 420, but again it was someone from out of town. It appeared the biker had been speeding and lost control.

Brooke had taken a four-week vacation after that crazy day when Joe had to come get her. It was winding down, with three weeks already gone, and she would need to decide what she was going to do. She had only gone out to take Frankie to school and to go visit her mom.

Now that she was free during the day, she stayed longer at her mom's house. Joe seemed happy for her that she was getting in all that free time, and he had continued to amaze her.

On her way back home, Shirley called.

"Hi gorgeous!" Brooke answered.

"Ha, I think not. How's it going?" Shirley asked.

"I am good, just left my mom's house. She is doing really well. I am so happy for her!"

"That's awesome. I know you deserve good things as much as you have gone through lately."

"Hmmmm, well I don't know about deserving good. I can't believe they still haven't figured out who shot those people at the park!" Brooke answered.

"I know you hardly ever look at social media, but the whole town is really coming down on the Chief. He is getting a lot of nasty feedback online as a result of the unsolved murders."

"I hate it for him. I know he is doing everything he can to try and solve it." Brooke said with a twinge of sadness.

"Well hopefully, that is about to change. My dog groomer's husband, who works at the jail, told her that they had some big leads and expected an arrest soon."

"Oh good. I am just ready for things to go back to normal."

"Have you heard anything from Tom?"

"No, not at all, since the day I met him at the old swimming hole. I still can't get over everything going on at his business."

"Yeah, me either. That is a lot of shit!" Shirley answered.

"I am just thankful that everything is out in the open now, for me and Joe. It's a relief not having to hide the affair. Joe has taken so much of the blame. I have tried to remind him it was my choice and I should have said no. I am grateful that we are able to communicate better now."

Shirley didn't answer, as she really wasn't sold completely on Joe's new attitude.

"He is still on good behavior, and it doesn't seem to be an act. We talk about our relationship now. Anyways, I bet Reece is excited about going away for spring break."

Brooke and Shirley continued talking about next week being spring break for the boys. Frankie was going to his Grandparent's house about an hour away. Joe's mom had called daily, making plans of all the things they wanted to do. Shirley was planning on going to Florida with her son for the week. Shirley had been disappointed that Frankie couldn't go with them, but she understood.

After she got off the phone with Shirley, Brooke pulled down her drive. Once she got inside, she was reading the local news feed on her phone and realized it was April 6, almost three months since the murders, and the days had flown by since.

Brooke was so grateful her life was finally peaceful. She figured Tom had worked things out with his work. She snuggled on the couch and closed her eyes. Her mind still wandering until she fell asleep.

While she slept, things were going crazy on the other side of town. News vans filled the streets again near the police station. The Chief was trying to prepare for the next few hours. The news had leaked that they were making an arrest today for the three murders.

His sergeants were out now making the arrest. He remained in the office, trying to type up his statement. He promised he would make the statement by two p.m. today. One thing the Chief knew after all these years of law, sometimes you just didn't know who was capable of committing terrible crimes.

The Chief started typing his statement. He wanted this to be his own words. This community was his heart. He was sad. The evidence was now overwhelming. It didn't sit right with him, but facts don't lie. He typed until he was satisfied. Today would change this community. It would be losing one of its own. He made sure his words respected this individual's family. The suspect's family always take the fall along with the guilty party, and they have no choice. The community would judge the family, even though they hadn't done anything wrong.

When Brooke woke up, she quickly grabbed her phone to look at the time. She hadn't known how long she had slept. She was relieved to find out that she still had a couple of hours before Frankie got off the bus. She decided to turn the TV on and flip through to see if anything good was on.

Every local station was showing the front of the police station here in Willowville. They were all awaiting the press conference that the Chief had promised.

Apparently, an arrest had been made. The news stations showed some videos that had been previously recorded of a police car driving to the back of the station with someone in the back. A jacket was wrapped around the person's face to hide their identity.

Now the cameras were back focused on the front of the station where the Chief would speak. Brooke's stomach turned. This brought all of it back. The man in her mirror, the guilt of her relationship with Tom, being at the park when she shouldn't have been, and the three victims.

She started to shake. She jumped up and yelled as the front door opened. It was Joe. He came over and hugged her. Before he could ask, he saw the television screen. The picture showed the front of the police station with one of the reporters recapping. Someone had been arrested for the murders of Ray Harper and the Parkers.

"Brooke, it is going to be okay, honey. Look, they are saying that they have arrested the killer. You should feel safer knowing they are off the street."

Brooke shook her head and told him, "I will just be glad when this is all over."

"It's about to be, sweetheart." Joe went and started coffee while they waited for the Chief.

The news station was showing pictures of the Parkers and of Ray Harper. The images were a terrible reminder to Brooke of everything that had happened.

When the Chief walked out, he was surprised by how many people were there. He walked over and stood at the podium, looking out at all the cameras and the reporters. He knew what he had to do but wasn't feeling good about it. He was visibly nervous.

He adjusted the microphone. He prayed for strength. He needed God to guide him through this.

"Ladies and Gentlemen, we appreciate all the thoughts and prayers that you have given our community. We also would like to thank everyone who called in tips. It has taken longer than we intended, but we wanted to be sure we caught the right person."

He paused before he continued. "I can report today that an arrest has been made. It is with a heavy heart that I must report that the suspect is a local. We made the arrest approximately an hour ago. Thomas Adcock has been arrested for triple homicide, of Ray Harper, Terry Parker, and Julie Parker."

Before he could continue, the reporters immediately started yelling questions at him.

He shook his head no, as he told them, "I am not going to be answering any questions today. We are going to follow the guidelines to ensure a fair trial."

The Chief turned and headed back into the station.

Tears rolled down Brooke's cheeks, as she watched him walk away on the television screen. Joe tensed beside her. She realized he was watching her. She then knew he was worried that she was crying for Tom, since she had an affair with him.

"Joe, I am not crying about Tom because of our relationship. I am crying for his family and his life. He has children. I also am scared! I need to let the police know that I was there with him. I don't think he could have murdered anyone."

Her phone started to ping. Shirley was sending multiple text messages. Joe looked at the phone and she was sure he was looking to verify who was texting her.

"Brooke, I just hate that this hurts you. But I must ask, do you still want to be with Tom?" He asked her.

"No Joe, I only want you and what we have now. I have always wanted our family. I believe that you want it now too."

Surprisingly to Brooke, Joe had tears rolling down his cheeks now as well. She couldn't remember a time that he had been so vulnerable.

She leaned over and kissed him. "I love you, Joe. I hate that I broke my promise of commitment to you. I am sorry that my actions may now hurt Frankie. I have hurt our family. However, I am so grateful that it brought us closer."

He held her tightly until the front door opened. Frankie came running in.

Frankie shouted as he came through the room. "They found the killer!"

She jumped again and realized she had forgotten to get him from the bus stop. Her nerves were shot. He was chatting a mile a minute.

"All the kids on the bus were talking about it!"

Joe hopped up from the couch and changed the subject, "Who wants to ride four-wheelers?"

It worked because Frankie went screaming yes through the hall to his room.

"Stay here at the house, honey. I will take Frankie out for a while." Joe looked completely comfortable taking control of things.

"Let me fix you another cup of coffee before I take him riding for a couple of hours. Get yourself together, honey. We will figure it out. I will go with you tomorrow to the police station. Yes, everyone will know about the affair, so we need to be prepared. Also, we need to talk to Frankie and explain things. I know you said that Tom left before you, but do you think he went back? Anyways, we can talk when I get back. I love you, and we can make it through this."

He kissed her forehead and headed to the kitchen. Her mind was spinning. The affair would be the talk of the town. Brooke knew Joe was right, they would have to tell Frankie. Her tears fell harder. She was so ashamed of herself.

Frankie flew by her, heading out the door. Luckily, he passed without even a glance in her direction. Joe came back in with a cup of coffee. She wiped her face with her sweatshirt sleeve.

She started to say Frankie's name, but Joe touched his finger to her lips. "Brooke, we got this, together we can get through anything."

Chapter 17

AMY AND HER FATHER-IN-LAW, David, stood in the living room. They were both upset from watching Tom be arrested and now they were staring at the television. Amy had calmed down just long enough to hear the Chief's statement. She immediately began screaming. David was crying too, as well as trying to console Amy.

She continued to scream, "This is all my fault. I should have helped Tom."

"Amy, we must remain strong. I don't believe our boy could do that kind of thing."

He shook when Amy said, "But he did."

David was certain she must have meant something else. He texted his wife and let her know what was happening. Sylvia was at their home along with Tom's girls. She had checked them out of school early, so they wouldn't know what was happening.

Tonight, David would have to tell the girls, but he and Sylvia wanted them to have a few more hours. They also didn't want them to hear through strangers what was happening. Sylvia had convinced them to turn off their phones - technically she had bribed them with shopping money. They had grumbled, but Granny had made a deal they couldn't refuse.

Reporters had now surrounded Tom's house. Amy paced and cried. David was dialing Tom's personal attorney.

Stan was on his way to the jailhouse.

"The evidence they have is circumstantial. Yes, Tom had been at the park but had already left and headed home. For now, Tom has only been accused of embezzlement by his company, not formally charged. David, I should have Tom out on bail, hopefully by tomorrow."

As David was relaying Stan's conversation to Amy, she collapsed. He could not wake her. He cursed as he dialed 9-1-1. He gave the operator the address. Amy was breathing but still unconscious. Time stopped for David. His son had been arrested, and his daughter-in-law had collapsed on the floor.

David was sitting on the floor with his phone in hand, next to Amy. She was still unconscious.

The emergency operator asked multiple times, "Is she still breathing?"

"Stop asking me that! If she stops, I will tell you. But you are scaring me to death, thinking that she may stop breathing."

"You are doing great, Mr. Adcock, just stay with me."

"How close is the ambulance? Damn, it's taking forever!"

The sirens blared loudly as the emergency vehicles pulled in, but the sound gave him relief. He was no longer alone in this. The EMT guy that came in first was a very close family friend. He immediately went to work on Amy. Her pulse was weak. Everyone there knew that Tom had just been arrested.

Within the next 15 minutes, the reporters were eating up the activities around the house. An ambulance and firetruck were now at the scene. Someone was being loaded into the ambulance, they reported. An older man was climbing in the ambulance with them.

One of the news reporters said it looked like a woman on the gurney. The sirens faded as they drove out of distance. Meanwhile, Amy remained unconscious on the ride to the hospital. The hospital had staff ready for her when they entered.

David sat down in the waiting room and texted Sylvia. David's mind was racing. His son had been arrested for murder and was facing criminal charges for embezzlement. His daughter-in-law, whom he loved like a daughter, was being seen by a medical staff in the emergency room. His wife was home alone with his soon to be heartbroken granddaughters. He prayed for all of them while he waited.

He had asked the front desk multiple times if there was any news on Amy. Each time they responded, "Not yet. We will let you know when you can go back."

David was surprised to see his wife walk in about an hour later. She grabbed him, and they hugged for what seemed like forever. Both of them were crying.

"Oh, David. I am crushed that Tom has been arrested, and when you told me about Amy, I couldn't stand it any longer, I wanted to be here with you. I know you wanted us to talk to the girls together, but I went ahead and told them. I didn't want them to hear the news from someone else."

"The girls are devastated, and they don't understand what is going on, but I just told them that I don't understand it all either."

Sylvia looked down as she whispered. "I just assured them that everything would be ok. The girls begged to come here so they could check on their mom. They are waiting in the car."

"It's okay, darling. Unfortunately, I haven't been told anything yet." David uttered.

Before they could decide what to do next, a nurse appeared. Dr. Tyler wanted to meet with them. The nurse led them to the family waiting room for the private consultation.

Dr. Tyler came in soon after and greeted them both. "Amy's conscious now, but she is in shock. We believe she has suffered a mental breakdown, but we will know more after we run more tests."

"She is being moved to the mental health floor, and you can come back to visit her after she is settled in. I recommend that you all wait until the following morning hours. Visitation is from nine a.m. until eleven a.m."

They got in the car and let the girls know that their mom was stable for now.

"Dr. Tyler said we can come back in the morning to visit your mom. They need to run more tests. They weren't able to give us much information." David informed his granddaughters.

"What will happen to Dad now?" Lucy asked.

Sylvia started to answer, but Addy interrupted.

"What's going to happen to Mom?" Addy's voice was cracking. She was scared and couldn't understand any of this.

Lucy continued talking, "I just don't understand why Dad would have been arrested for something he didn't do?"

"What if Mom doesn't make it?" Addy cried.

The whole ride home was filled with questions, which no one knew the answers to.

Chapter 18

Dr. Tyler walked out of Amy's room the following morning. He told the nurse to let the family know he wanted to speak to them before they visited Amy.

David was at Tom's house when the nurse called him. He had gone there to grab a few of Amy's things before they visited with her at the hospital. Sylvia and Tom's girls waited back at his house. He hurried along and looked for Amy's phone. He noticed she had gotten a new phone as he remembered her screen had been cracked for years.

He grabbed some of Amy's clothes and house shoes, a pair he had seen her wearing often. He knew Sylvia could go shopping for her later, if needed. He had no idea how long they would keep Amy at the hospital.

David thought about the previous night, when they told Lucy and Addy everything that was happening with their dad and their mom. Both girls had remained strong even through their tears, but this was terrifying to them. They both agreed that their dad was innocent and seemed sure their dad would get out of this. For now, they were more concerned with their mother's health.

David checked the front door locks and exited out the back door. He walked down the trail to a neighbor's house, where he had parked his car to avoid the media trucks that were still camped out in front of Tom's house.

He grabbed his family and when they all arrived at the hospital, they were escorted down a long hall to an office where they now waited. The girls were visibly shaken. Both of Tom's parents felt it was important to include them. They couldn't protect them from all of this anymore.

Dr. Tyler came in and sat beside Lucy on the small couch. He looked at each of the girls, unsure if he wanted to have this conversation with them present. David assured him that the girls have been told of everything going on.

The doctor's eyebrows raised, but Mrs. Adcock nodded yes. "Everything."

Dr. Tyler stated that Amy's physical health was stable. Her vitals remained strong but they faltered if Amy got upset. After testing throughout the night and again this morning, he was pretty certain Amy had suffered a nervous breakdown yesterday.

"She will be placed on some medications to help her and will have daily counseling." He suggested that they all remain positive with Amy while visiting.

Dr. Tyler led the family down to Amy's room.

"Mom!" Addy ran over to Amy's bed.

"Hey, honey." Amy looked tired. She hugged both girls.

"You gave me quite a scare, young lady," David said as he came over to get a hug from Amy.

Amy raised her eyebrows, "I guess, but I am not sure what happened."

"You passed out on me. Thankfully, I was there and called 9-1-1. I'm sure it was just all the stress you and Tom have been under recently." David replied.

She looked puzzled. Sylvia came over to stand next to the bed. She put her hand on Amy's hand to comfort her.

"Where is Tom?" Amy questioned her.

Everyone in the room seemed confused, unsure why she asked for Tom, since she should know he was in jail. The doctor walked over to the bed and began asking Amy questions.

"Amy, do you mind if I ask you a few questions?"

"I don't mind you asking, but I really don't even know why I am here."

"That's ok. Your body is just tired. Can you tell me what day it is?" He asked as he studied her chart.

She paused. "No, I feel like I have been asleep forever. I am not sure what day it is."

Amy looked cautiously at everyone standing around her, and suddenly, her head turned quickly to the girls. "Oh Lucy, when did you get your long hair cut off?"

Lucy frowned, "Mom, I got my hair cut off over a year ago? What are you talking about?"

Dr. Tyler interrupted before anyone else could say anything.

"I think your mom is exhausted. So let's head out so she can get some rest. If you guys can follow me out." He requested.

"Wait, we just got here?" Addy said.

"I really wish everyone could stay." Amy was getting annoyed – her family had just arrived.

The family hugged Amy goodbye and followed the doctor to the hallway.

"Can you tell us what is going on?" David asked Dr. Tyler.

"I want to run further tests. It seems Amy is experiencing some confusion."

"Well, she's not the only one! How did she forgot about me cutting ten inches of my hair off last year?" Lucy injected.

Addy was sobbing as they left the hospital, more clueless than when they arrived.

The following morning, the doctor met with David and Sylvia. He had asked that they leave the girls at home until they talked.

"Well, I've got some bad news, and I don't know how to make this any easier. We ran some more tests, after Amy's confusion episode yesterday. Amy did experience a mental breakdown. As a result, it appears the events have triggered Dissociative Amnesia."

He then explained in further detail. "That's when the brain blocks out memories to prevent pain. She has little to no memory of the last year and a half.

"Amnesia?" Sylvia challenged him. "That seems impossible. She knew all of us yesterday."

"Yes. It seems that Amy does remember everyone. Amnesia doesn't always mean you can't remember anything. Sometimes it is just a section of the memory that is missing." He replied.

He then went into detail about the condition.

"It often results from stress and trauma. These stints of amnesia usually come on suddenly and can last hours, days, or sometimes months. We will monitor her and she will continue counseling, hopefully that will help her improve and possibly even regain those memories."

He advised them to act normal when they saw her.

"Do not mention any of the recent events going on. You don't want to make Amy have a setback. In some cases, you help a patient with amnesia by telling them stories they can't remember, that isn't the case here, those memories caused her to have a mental breakdown. For now, we just want her brain to relax and heal."

"I brought her phone. Do I need to hold onto it instead?" David asked.

"Let's wait for now."

They all agreed and followed the doctor to Amy's room. Amy looked like a child lying in the hospital bed. She smiled as they walked in. She hugged them and held onto them for a while. She apologized to them for getting so emotional and being confused.

"Where's Tom and the girls?"

Dr. Tyler took charge of the situation.

"It appears your husband and daughters couldn't come this morning."

"I just miss them all so badly. David, please tell them I love them, and I hope they can come next time."

She looked at Dr. Tyler, "Will I be able to leave soon?"

"For now, you need to stay here. Your blood pressure and heart rate are causing some problems, when you get excited or upset. We have to get that under control and then you can go home with your family."

The Adcocks visited until their time was up. By the end of the visit, the nurse came in and gave Amy some medicine. She fell asleep soon afterward.

David and Sylvia now sat out in the waiting room, processing their visit and the information they had been given by the doctor before they headed home. Neither could believe this was happening to Amy. It had been stressful sitting there with her, but unable to talk with her about anything.

"I don't understand how Amy has amnesia all of a sudden," Sylvia whispered.

"I don't either, sweetheart. I feel like I am stuck in a nightmare that just won't end. What else is going to happen to this family?"

On their way home, David had a text from the attorney. **The bond hearing is set for two o'clock this afternoon.**

David got home and dressed to go to the courthouse. Sylvia sat on the bed crying. She told him she was scared and worried for this family. Their world seemed to be falling apart around them. He hugged her, and they said a prayer together. He suggested she take the girls to their cabin in the mountains for the remainder of the week.

"It will get the girls away from here for a few days."

"I don't feel right leaving in the middle of all of this. I want the girls to be away from this too, but do you think leaving is the answer? Are you going to be able to handle everything?"

"I will be fine. I love you. Soon this will all be over. I promise." David answered, fearing this might be the first promise he ever broke to Sylvia.

"Once Amy is better and Tom is cleared, we can all go together on a long vacation."

The courtroom was packed. It was full of news reporters and several of the locals. Many of the locals came up to David and greeted him as he entered. He felt out of place here. It was chaos to him. He tried to figure out where he needed to be and finally took a seat behind Stan.

David looked over to the side door as it opened. Two officers escorted Tom out to the table with his attorney. The District Attorney, whom David knew as well, sat at the table on the other side, with the Chief sitting right behind him.

The Bailiff called, "All rise, court is now in session," as the Judge walked in.

"You may be seated," the Judge stated once he had taken his place.

The Judge went over the rules of his courtroom. He advised the whole room what the procedure for today would be.

"Will the State Counsel, please present the charges against the defendant in this case?"

"Your Honor, the state charges Thomas Adcock with first degree triple homicide of Terry Parker, Julie Parker, and Ray Harper."

"Defendant, please stand and state your full name for the court."

Tom stood but was shaking and his face was full of fear.

"Thomas Adcock."

"To the charge of triple homicide, what is your plea?"

Tom's body was shaking, and his voice cracked.

"Your honor, I plead Not Guilty."

The room buzzed with chatter and the judge demanded silence in the courtroom. He dismissed Tom and told him to be seated.

Tom's attorney then stood and went to the podium.

"Your honor, Thomas Adcock deserves to be released on bail. He has been a resident of this community his entire life. He has been an outstanding citizen with a clear record. We request that you grant bond with house arrest, until the court trial can begin. The District Attorney has no real evidence that ties Thomas to the case. Yes, he was at the park, along with probably more than thirty other people, but he gave his reason for being there. Yes, there is an active investigation by his company due to missing money, but no formal charges have been filed. The police don't even have a weapon. We appreciate your ability to see that the evidence provided by the state has a lot of cracks and is based on circumstantial evidence."

He then went back to the table with Tom.

The judge thanked him and called the attorney for the state. He approached the podium and greeted the judge.

"Thank you for your time, your honor. We would like for bond to be denied for just the very reasons that were previously stated. Thomas Adcock has many resources in his hometown. A town that is filled with people that would help him in any way they can as they feel he's innocent. Just the fact it took so long to make the arrest proves that his peers think highly of him."

Then after his dramatic pause he continued. "Tom's bond with the community has outweighed justice. Thomas Adcock is a liar, and we have proof of his guilt. We also feel that he is a flight risk. The holes in the evidence that were referenced are false. We request that Thomas Adcock remain in jail. We appreciate your intelligence and judgement in separating familiarity with professionalism. Our separate request is that the trial be moved to an area that will not be biased. Thomas has been charged with three counts of murder and is under investigation for embezzlement. Please deny the bond request."

The judge requested a short recess. While he was gone, Tom was escorted from the courtroom. Several men had gathered around David. His family was loved. These men were the same men he sat with in Church every Sunday morning. They all had come to support the family.

A while later, Tom was escorted back to the court room and sat down again with his attorney. When the Judge came back, the court was told to rise. David watched his son and prayed for him to be released.

The Judge cleared his throat, "I have reviewed the documents associated with this case. I have gone over the evidence that has been provided and the statements provided. I am forced for now, based on this evidence, to deny bond. Thomas Adcock, you will remain jailed until your trial. Also, I will file to have the case transferred to a different court."

The crowd erupted, the judge raised his voice as he told them, "Silence, you will not disrespect my court or my decision. If I hear another word, you will be arrested."

Tom sat paralyzed by fear.

After Tom was escorted from the courtroom, Tom's attorney approached David.

"Sir, I am so sorry. I will be meeting Tom later today for a consult, and hope that you can attend the meeting."

"Of course, I will be there. What happens now?"

"We can discuss our next steps today with Tom." David felt sick, and his heart was breaking. He now had to go home and let Tom's girls and his wife know that bond had been denied.

Chapter 19

AT THE POLICE STATION, things were hectic and emotions were high as most of the cops knew Tom well and they were all in shock. They had all been shaken by this whole ordeal. The Chief agreed with them but also said justice comes first. He walked into his office and sat at his desk. His assistant knocked on his door. She was upset by everything happening.

"Are you okay? Poor Tom and Amy - I knew them well as we all graduated together." She asked.

"No, but this is my job. Living under this oath, I must do it, no matter if it hurts."

"I spoke to Tom's father earlier, and Amy is still hospitalized but stable. Also, Brooke Smith called and scheduled an appointment with you for this afternoon," the assistant informed him.

The Chief was fond of Brooke. He had been very close to her father – he missed seeing his friend.

"Can you please hold my calls for the remainder of the day, if possible?" He asked his assistant.

She assured him she could handle everyone. She walked sadly from his office.

The Chief was unsure what Brooke was coming in for. He just prayed nothing bad had happened to her or her family. He thought of her mother, but he had heard from mutual friends that she was doing better.

He looked at the office calendar and saw that Tom's attorney had scheduled a meeting with Tom. He had been surprised that the bond request was denied. He suspected his slowness of the arrest hadn't helped the matter. The Chief didn't think Tom was a flight risk at all, and he also wasn't convinced Tom was guilty.

An hour later, Brooke and Joe entered his office. He greeted them both and gave Brooke a hug.

"You are a sight for sore eyes," he told her.

She smiled but quickly responded. "You might change your mind about that."

He frowned at her.

Brooke then told him, "We heard out in the front that Tom had not been released for bond. That's terrible for him and his family."

"They have rules that they must follow, Brooke. It sucks, but that's how it works," the Chief explained.

Brooke went straight into why she was there.

"I was at the park on the night of the murders."

The Chief stopped her, "Brooke, a lot of folks were there. We are sure that over half of them have not reported it. You are not in trouble for that, if that's what you thought."

She looked sad as she spoke, "I was there with Tom."

The Chief jerked. "What do you mean, with Tom?"

She whispered as she told him about her brief affair with Tom. She explained that she had only seen Tom once after that night.

"I also know all about the embezzlement stuff with his company. I had hoped that he had been able to clear it all up."

The Chief looked from her to Joe. He watched her husband's face, and it never changed. He was impressed with her husband coming here in these circumstances to support her.

"What time did you leave Brooke? Did Tom leave at the same time?"

She wasn't sure of the exact time, and she ended up having to go back to town for gas.

"Maybe nine-twenty, nine-thirty, I am not sure. Tom left before me."

Brooke then told the Chief about the man in the orange toboggan. The Chief laughed inappropriately as he pulled an orange toboggan from his desk drawer.

"Like this? Half the men in our town have an orange toboggan, Brooke. I am sure your dad had one. Most of them have it for safety when they are walking in the woods, getting ready for hunting."

She hadn't thought of that.

"I am sure it's the same man each time that I have seen him. I am positive that he isn't a local. He even followed me once, actually he chased me."

The Chief assured her he didn't think that was anything to worry about.

"I know you very well Brooke, I think you have just got yourself worked up based on everything that had happened at the park."

She smiled and hoped he was right, but it sure had seemed like the same man.

"Brooke, the charges against Tom are backed by evidence. In fact, this affair now makes Tom seem even more likely to be guilty. He was cheating on his wife, his partner was shot, Tom was there, and is facing embezzlement charges from his company."

Brooke agreed that things looked bad, but she had never seen any signs from Tom that anything other than Amy's depression was wrong in his life.

"Did you know that Amy has been hospitalized?" The Chief asked.

"Yes, and I feel horrible." Brooke felt so guilty for her role in this, she felt to blame for Amy's condition.

On the other side of the station, Tom, his father, and Stan sat gathered around a table. "The embezzlement charges will be tried before the murder trial. So, it gives us more time to squash that charge, then the DA's office would be set with very little evidence."

"This is unbelievable, I have never even gotten a speeding ticket and I am sitting in jail for murder!"

"Tom, being at the wrong place at the wrong time, does not make you guilty. The notes from the DA show that you knew the Parkers would be here in Willowville that night?"

"Who is the witness that claimed that? I swear I didn't know." Tom seemed defeated. "Am I allowed to know?"

The attorney's head dropped as he spoke. "Amy, your wife."

David opened his mouth, but no words came out. He hadn't told Tom yet about Amy's condition.

"Amy?" Tom was confused as he asked. "That's stupid! Why would Amy have said that?"

"The Chief had requested she come into the station for questioning. He asked her about the time you came home, and when asked about knowing the Parkers would be in town, she had said yes."

"Why the hell did Amy talk to the Chief? She didn't mention it to me. It makes no sense, and how would she have known they were in town?" Tom was yelling and he felt blinded by confusion.

"Tom, stop." David interrupted him, worried about people hearing his confusion and anger. "Amy's in the hospital."

David explained what had happened the day before, when Amy collapsed and was rushed to the hospital. He told them about her diagnosis. Tom was silent. He was caught in an avalanche and couldn't stop it. God must be punishing me for the affair, Tom thought.

"Your mom and I have told the girls everything that's going on."

Tom frowned and looked disappointed.

"How did they take the news about the affair?"

His father was shocked.

"Affair? What affair?" David jerked in response to Tom's remark.

"Dad, I am so sorry. I thought you had heard. I messed up!"

He explained about meeting up with Brooke at the rally and how things had just progressed.

"I confessed to Amy about it, so I thought she would have told you. I ended things with Brooke, and I am trying to fix things with Amy. Do you think Amy said that I knew the Parkers were here, to hurt me?"

By the end of the meeting, things looked bleak. The attorney was planning on going out to P & A Tech the next day. He wanted to follow up on the status of the money transactions. They needed to know what computer had been used in the crimes. David was still visibly upset. He couldn't believe that Tom had cheated on Amy.

Chapter 20

STAN STOOD IN THE P & A Tech office and thought about the past week. He had arranged to meet with the office team and the office attorney. He had flown in early that morning.

This was the most difficult case he had ever worked on. He usually knew when a client was lying, which made it easier. A liar could be guilty. Tom didn't seem to be lying, but the evidence was piling up against him. He truly didn't think Tom was guilty, but there was nothing to help him dispute the charges.

John had come up front to meet him. The others were getting ready, and they would start the meeting soon. They chatted about the weather and small talk as they headed to the conference room.

This meeting was so important for Tom's case. If they could get this embezzlement stuff dropped, he felt like they would have to drop the murder charges. The tech team had pushed to find the computer that had been used in the crime. Stan was trying to remain positive. The information from the computer used could be the key to all of this.

Once they had gathered around the table, the tech team manager stood up. He introduced himself to Stan, Tom's attorney, again.

"It took us a while to trace down the computer, but we did find the IP address information and tracked it to a computer owned by our company. Unfortunately, the computer was assigned to Tom."

The group flinched at the words.

"It appears that another computer was sent to Tom in February of the previous year. Tom had requested it as he claimed his previous one had crashed. The Inventory Department had sent a new computer and a shipping box to return the damaged one. The broken computer was never received back."

"This makes no sense..." Stan was trying to comprehend the information.

The tech lead continued explaining. "The process for a computer exchange is to ship the new computer to someone and a return box for the old one."

Everyone here, except for the two attorneys, knew the process.

"In this case, the previous computer was never received back. That was the computer used for all the money transactions to the offshore account. The status notes from last year had been entered as non-returned for this computer. The inventory team figured since Tom was the boss, they didn't need to follow up with him. We don't have the computer but we do know it was used in the money transfers."

All of the men in the room were quiet. The office attorney, Steve, spoke first, "This changes everything. We will have to proceed with filing charges against Tom. I am truly disappointed and shocked."

"We owe it to Terry and the company to bring justice. I am disappointed as well. Tom always treated us all like family. I guess we didn't know what he was doing. We will help with anything from our side that needs to be done." John agreed with Steve.

"Gentlemen, I will talk to my client. For now, we are requesting that you guys do not make any changes to his company until it is processed through the trial and he is formally found guilty." Stan asked of the group.

They all agreed the company would stay within the status quo until the case was tried.

Stan called David from his car when he left.

"David, it's Stan. How's everything going? Amy?"

"Everyone's hanging in there. Amy is stable but is still missing part of her memories. How did things go there?" David replied.

"I can't lie to you, it's bad. The computer used in the crime belonged to Tom."

"That can't be true! I don't believe it. My son may have cheated on his wife, but I don't believe he was stealing from his own company. I also don't believe he would take someone's life."

Stan told him he didn't either. "I usually don't say whether I think my client is guilty, but this doesn't add up. He could have sold the company for more than enough to cover the amount stolen. The crime was too neat, a criminal checklist of what not to do. Tom, for sure, wouldn't have used his own computer! Hell, he was in the tech world. He would have known better. I also believe Tom didn't know about the Parkers being in Willowville. It sucks even worse because we can't ask Amy what she meant when she told the police they did know. Do the doctors know how long before her memory returns?"

"Unfortunately, they have no idea. What if it never returns?" he asked before Stan had to hang up for another call coming in.

Sylvia had been devastated, as well, when David had called and shared the news with her. The girls were enjoying the cabin.

"I am headed to Tom's house now to clean out his refrigerator and to check on everything. I want it all taken care of when Tom and Amy return home."

David refused to accept that they both might not come home. Tom was in so much trouble. He was grateful to be blessed to have the money to help, since Tom's assets would now be frozen.

Chapter 21

Over the next few weeks, Brooke stayed home as much as possible. Her employer had been very understanding and given her all the time she needed off. She had pulled Frankie from school, and he was doing his work remotely.

Frankie was doing well and had handled their talk better than Brooke expected. It was a lot to drop on a kid his age. The news outlets had been alerted to the affair. They had found an old photo of her and were using it on television with the stories.

Frankie had been shocked but was actually more upset with his dad. He blamed Joe instead of his mom, and Brooke was surprised by this. At one point, Frankie had actually looked at his dad and said this was all his fault because he had been so mean to his mom all these years.

Both Brooke and Joe had been surprised by his remark. Joe seemed embarrassed, and Brooke was sad. She thought she had been protecting Frankie better. Frankie asked if they were going to get a divorce now. They told him no. Joe said he was trying to be a better husband, a better father, and overall, a better man.

Joe did all the duties that required leaving the house. Reporters were constantly camped out at the end of their driveway now. Brooke was enjoying the time with Frankie but she was going stir-crazy. She blamed herself for ruining Frankie's life. They were prisoners in their own home because of her actions.

But today, that was going to change. She was going to take Frankie out today. Shirley had agreed to come get them. Joe was worried but agreed. He was going to distract the reporters so that they could sneak out.

When Shirley arrived, she commented, "Those fucking reporters are sick, like vultures out there just waiting for something to die."

She hugged Brooke – she missed her so much. They hadn't had alone time in so long. Brooke missed their time too. They decided to meet Joe's parents to drop off the boys and then find somewhere off the grid to eat. Joe had made the arrangements with his parents.

Shirley and Brooke sat at a Mexican restaurant far away from their hometown. They both ordered margaritas. They laughed and cried throughout the meal.

"Things with Joe are still going well. He seems like a new man." Brooke shared.

"A wolf in sheep's clothing? I'm sorry, Brooke, I shouldn't have said that. I am happy that he has stepped up and has been so supportive."

Brooke laughed. The margaritas seemed to be working.

"I know you are worried. I loved Joe taking those reporters on a wild goose chase. When he yelled at them to follow him, and that he would give a statement, was too funny. Not one reporter had stayed near my driveway."

"Yep, as soon as they went one way, we went the other." Shirley sipped her drink.

Later as they drove back into Willowville, Brooke wasn't ready to go home yet. She wanted to grab some snacks from the grocery store. As they parked, they noticed the store looked pretty empty. The boys decided to stay in the car. Brooke was still a little buzzed from her two margaritas. As they headed over to the chip aisle, Brooke stood loading some stuff in her buggy. She had promised the boys that tonight, Joe would build a fire, and they could make s'mores. Both boys loved that idea.

As Brooke turned, she came face to face with Clara Edwards. Clara had been snotty to them in school. She seemed to soften a little as they got older, but now she was looking at Brooke with disgust.

"Homewrecker! You should be sitting in that jail with Tom. Poor Amy. And now, because of you, she is stuck in a hospital. ALL because of you!" Her words echoed around Brooke.

Brooke's face turned red. She couldn't speak.

Shirley's voice now echoed, "Clara Edwards, you rotten whore, shouldn't you be at the motel with your husband cooking meth?"

Clara's face was now just as red. Everyone in town had heard about her husband getting caught and arrested at the motel, making drugs.

"I guess you are just jealous, since your husband went and found someone else! Now, you don't have a husband to go home to, right Shirley?"

At that, Clara turned and stormed off.

Shirley and Brooke stood in the middle of the aisle looking at each other. The store was silent. Moments passed before Brooke broke down laughing.

Shirley's laughter followed as Brooke continued. The sound of their laughter filled the store, it was so loud.

They both had sat down in the floor still laughing until an employee came over and was watching them. The young employee was a familiar face as she had worked there for a couple of years.

"Clean up on aisle 7!" Shirley called. Brooke snorted.

Then they both apologized to the employee and made their way to check out. They paid and left the store.

Later as they told Joe about the encounter, he wasn't laughing.

"Dammit, Brooke, you guys should be on your best behavior. With everything that is going on, you don't need someone seeing you behaving childishly!"

"Boo! I don't care what anyone thinks anymore! I am not going to hide anymore! Everyone in this town has a past that isn't perfect. I am done feeling like the lowest human ever."

"What about Frankie, don't you care what people say to him? I am not trying to beat you up, I just want you to be mindful."

"I'm sorry. I will just be glad when school is out in a few weeks. Hopefully, by then things should calm down."

"Geez Joe, cut her some slack. I agree that no one wants Frankie to suffer, but an affair isn't the worst thing in the world. Brooke can't pay for Tom's wrongdoings." Shirley said.

Joe's head turned quickly to look at Shirley. He smiled, "So does that mean you think he's guilty?"

Shirley nodded in agreement, "Yes, I do. Apparently, he had a ring of things going on. If it walks like a duck, and talks like a duck, it usually means it is a duck."

Brooke whispered, "It sure looks like he's guilty."

The two women sat on the porch, watching Joe and the boys play with the fire.

"I'm really sorry, Brooke. I was on the fence about Tom, but it sure seems stacked against him. I heard he knew the Parkers would be there at the park that night, with that and the embezzlement charges, he sure seems guilty."

Brooke didn't argue. She knew from all the details that had leaked – Tom appeared guilty. She hadn't seen that side of Tom. She really believed what they had shared was genuine and that he was a good person.

Brooke admitted to Shirley that she was eager to feel normal again. She looked over at Joe and the boys, and noticed Joe was watching her. She smiled at him.

Later Brooke lay in bed, tired of thinking. It had been too long of a time now to continue to beat herself up. Tomorrow she and Frankie would go to her mom's. It was time to take her life back. She would plan a vacation for them. If Joe couldn't take off work, she would ask Shirley and Reece to accompany them. The beach sounded like heaven to her.

Chapter 22

THE SMELL OF THE flowers in the hospital courtyard brought Amy joy. Summer was here. She enjoyed her walk out here every day now. She hated the blank spot in her memory and prayed daily for it to return.

Amy also hated and worried that she hadn't seen Tom in so long. She thought something must have happened to him. Otherwise he would be here to see her. Every time she asked about him though, someone changed the subject. She imagined the worst. Maybe they had both been in a car wreck, and that's why her memory was gone. Tom could be dead.

She started to feel a panic attack coming, so she practiced the breathing method that the counselor had taught her. She had been so surprised to learn that she was missing part of her memory.

The counselor had helped her narrow it down to almost a year and a half that was missing. She literally couldn't remember anything during that time. She remembered celebrating Christmas with the girls, but another Christmas had come and gone since then. She couldn't remember this past one.

She cried daily, missing the girls and Tom. She tried to do everything the counselor told her to do. She wanted to get better so that she could go home. She knew the panic attacks prevented her from being discharged. Her blood pressure would rise to a dangerous level, so she had to be monitored.

Amy closed her eyes as she enjoyed the heat from the sun and the smell of the flowers. She pictured snow falling and imagined she was driving, but couldn't place where. The snow was mixed with sleet.

Her father-in-law called her name, and the image was gone. She waved at him.

"Hey." She beamed at him like he was her own father. She needed him to be direct with her.

"David, is Tom dead? I have to know."

"Oh Amy, no. I promise you that Tom is not dead. He is just out of town. Right now, all you need to do is focus on getting yourself better."

"How are Lucy and Addy? I miss them all so much. I just want to go home."

Because of her medical condition, the girls had been limited to only weekend visits.

"I understand that you do. We all want you to be able to come home, but until Dr. Tyler thinks you are ready, it's best for you to be here. Just follow the program, and you will be home sooner than you think."

He smiled and patted her arm.

"I just need to see Tom," she said sadly.

Amy watched as another family came into the courtyard. This area was reserved for the mental health ward only.

David noticed the other family as well. He glanced at Amy.

"Don't worry, darling, everything will be okay."

David's mind was weak today with worry. He wanted to snap out of this nightmare they had been living. Formal charges had now been filed by P & A Tech against Tom for embezzlement. His son was sitting in jail for murder.

He was thankful that he was still able to visit with Tom. The local jail was giving them more visitation than the law allowed. Tom assured his father he was doing okay. He had friends that worked there, and they made sure he was treated well. Most of the guys he knew there didn't believe he was guilty.

The embezzlement charge had made things tougher, though. Tom told his father the truth had to come out - it just had to. He had sworn on his mother's life that he was not guilty. David believed he hadn't killed anyone or stolen any money, and it made him angry at the situation.

They had talked about his old computer that was broken. Tom assured his father that Amy had mailed it back for him. He clearly remembered the morning that she planned on mailing it, as he had been packing to leave on a trip that day. She had a huge panic attack. She left and returned about an hour or so later.

David sat and looked at Amy now and he wanted to ask her about the computer. He wanted her to remember and help figure this out. He knew she was trying. He also could see the counseling was helping her.

He loved Amy like she was his daughter. This was breaking them all. He stayed and chatted with Amy until visitation time was over and hugged her goodbye.

"We love you. You just need to stay strong and work on getting better."

"I love you guys too." She turned her head so that he couldn't see the tears forming in her eyes.

After David left, he started to drive towards Tom's house but decided to wait a while. He didn't know if the news crews would be there, and he didn't want to take the chance of running into them. He had seen some of their vans driving in the area on his way to the hospital this morning. He knew the embezzlement charges had stirred them up again. He wanted to scream at them, to just go away and leave his family alone.

He turned off the highway onto a back road. He decided to just drive for a while. He remembered when Tom was young, as an only child, he had been a good kid. In his opinion, Tom had become a great man. He knew in his heart Tom was innocent and he wanted to find a way to prove it.

He came to an old mill area and pulled off the road. He called Tom's attorney. They discussed the process for the new charges of embezzlement. There would not be a hearing to hear Tom's plea. For now, until they could find some new evidence, Tom would remain in jail.

The trial for the murders was set for November. The District Attorney was pushing for the Texas DA to start the embezzlement trial in the fall, since that charge had to be tried in Texas. The District Attorney, here in Georgia, would want to have the "guilty embezzlement verdict" on hand before the murder trial.

Stan told David, "We have two months to try and find something to clear Tom."

The attorney then brought up the broken computer. Tom insisted that he had packaged it up the morning after his new one arrived. He insisted that he had gotten Amy to drop the box off at the post office. She had told him that it had been sent.

"I will go by Tom's this evening to see if I can find the postal receipt from around that time." David offered.

He got back on the road and headed to his son's house. There was one news station van still sitting there, so he parked at his friend's house down the road from Tom's house. He went straight to Tom's office. Papers were scattered everywhere.

He knew that the district attorney had issued a search warrant. He was disgusted of the way they had left it. Tom deserved better than this. He spent the next few hours straightening up and going through all the papers. He couldn't find any postal receipts and he wondered, maybe they had been taken by the search team.

He went into Amy's office. It was neat and apparently perfectly organized. He did find a folder on her desk that was filled with receipts for groceries and household purchases. He noticed most of the purchases made in the last several months showed pick up or delivery.

Finally, he found a prior year file and there was one receipt from the right time frame, but it was mailed to Julie Parker at her home address. He assumed she and Amy had swapped Christmas presents late, maybe. He finally gave up and headed to his house.

Chapter 23

Brooke, Shirley, and the boys were heading to the beach. Joe hadn't been able to go and Brooke had secretly been glad. She was excited about having some girl time. It was only about a five-hour drive, and it had been filled with singing along with the radio and laughter. Both boys were so excited. Brooke was looking forward to a peaceful vacation. A week without any worry.

When they arrived, Brooke called Joe while out on the balcony. They chatted for a while, until the boys yelled that they wanted to head down to the beach. She hung up with Joe and told the boys to give her fifteen minutes to change. She also told them to get the sunscreen and towels ready.

When she came out, Shirley whistled, "Holy cow, you look amazing. I can't believe how skinny you have gotten!"

Brooke smiled and thanked her. Brooke chatted for a minute about how much everything had changed this last year. "One good thing is that I've lost all this weight."

The boys interrupted them and said, "Let's go," in unison.

The next few days flew by. The trip was so relaxing. It was one gorgeous day after another with the wind blowing off the water, and it felt so good. Brooke could smell the ocean and feel the sun beaming down on her. Shirley had fallen asleep, and the boys were building sandcastles.

Brooke watched Frankie as he played. She had put him in a horrible situation these last few months. If Tom had killed those people after she left, he deserved jail, but Frankie didn't deserve punishment for any of this. He was handling everything so well.

Frankie had talked to her about all of it, often. He really was more upset with Joe, than with her. She told Frankie she had made the choice to cheat, not Joe. He told her that he hated his dad. She had been taken aback by his statement.

"Oh, honey, you don't hate your dad. Being angry at someone doesn't mean you hate them."

"Dad is not a nice person, Mom."

"But things are better now, right? Your dad has been great these last several months."

Frankie had then said, "I don't believe he has really changed. I wish he would leave, and it could be just me and you. I saw how he treated you before, Mom."

She had spent another hour trying to sway him. Joe did seem to be sincere, but she wasn't fully there yet either. She thought about his behavior and actions over the months since the murders. He really was treating her like a partner now. Hopefully, she and Frankie would both believe it was real as time passed. She prayed with all her heart that Joe had changed and that it was sincere.

She looked now at Frankie's sweet face. At the same time, he caught her watching him.

"Mom, you are being a creep!" He joked as he busted out laughing.

They stayed for a few more hours and played in and out of the water until the boys finally decided they were starving. The day had flown by.

The next day Brooke and Shirley lay stretched out in the pool lounge chairs. The boys were sitting at a table nearby, eating their lunches. Brooke looked over to see Shirley watching the boys and she was smiling. A smile that Brooke hadn't seen on her in years.

"I've been a horrible friend to you lately, Shirley." Brooke frowned as she spoke. "I have been so caught up in my own mess these last six months, and I haven't even asked how you've been. I don't even know what you have going on in your life."

Brooke had noticed that her friend had lost some weight as well. She was glowing. Shirley seemed to have more pep in her step lately.

"Brooke," Shirley laughed, "Hush your mouth! You have been through so much for so long. You are my best friend, and I am so grateful for you."

Brooke loved seeing her this happy.

"I do have some news, though," Shirley teased.

Brooke's eyebrows raised as she spoke, "Good news?"

Shirley chuckled, "Yes, good news."

Shirley's laugh was contagious.

"Tell me!" Brooke had now sat up in her chair with her leg tapping.

"I have been chatting with someone."

Brooke's eyes were wide, "WHO? I need details!"

Shirley also sat up now, "Eric Stinson, he called me about a month ago."

Brooke was floored by this, "Eric? What did he say?"

Shirley told her that a number that showed up as unknown had called her. Brooke's mind skipped to her unknown number caller, but fortunately the calls had stopped.

"I thought it might be a reporter. They had been calling me because of our shared photos and such. When you blocked your social media accounts, they came after me."

Brooke immediately apologized.

"No honey, you're not responsible for them being vultures. I was surprised it was Eric, and then we just started chatting. We talked for almost two hours, that first call."

Brooke asked her about how he had been since discovering the dead woman at the park. Shirley told her that they had talked very little about that night. She knew it had upset him beyond words.

"We mostly just caught up on life. I've run into him several times over the last several years, with him coaching and working for the rec center. He has always been nice but very reserved. We would wave or say a quick hi to each other, unless we were chatting about the boys and how they were doing. Eric wants to take me out on a date. But I haven't said yes, yet."

Shirley blushed as she spoke.

"Also, just because I want you to know that I would never bad mouth you, Eric has mentioned the affair between you and Tom. He was really disappointed in you both. I did explain to him a little about your life with Joe before the murders. I'm really sorry if that bothers you."

Brooke shook her head. "No, it doesn't bother me. I am disappointed in myself. I never set out to hurt anyone. It stings that I have lost a lot of respect from people in our community." Brooke admitted.

They were interrupted as the boys came over. They wanted to go down to one of the arcades across the street from the condos. Everyone packed up and headed to the rooms to get ready.

Brooke grabbed Shirley's hand in the hall on the way up, "I think you should go out with Eric. I am so happy for you. You deserve a good guy."

They all headed out for the evening.

Later, Brooke sat on the balcony, drinking coffee, and listening to the waves. It was the last night of the trip. This place was magical to her. She wouldn't ever move out of Willowville because it was home, but seeing the beach once a year reminded her of how big the world was, and she loved it.

She thought of her daddy. Besides his death, this past year had been the hardest thing she had ever gone through. This week with Shirley and the boys had been so much fun and she had needed it, more than she realized.

Those boys were so full of life, but they had been through a lot because of their fathers. Thankfully they hadn't seemed affected as both were very kind and loving. The week had been filled with laughter and tears. Brooke had loved this time but was ready to get back home. She missed her mom.

She realized with a twinge of sadness that she hadn't missed Joe as much as she thought she would. Until this week, Brooke hadn't realized, even though Joe was being nice, the damage had been done. She still felt like she was walking on eggshells with him, and she couldn't be honest with him. Fear kept her from being all in with him. That made her sad. She was just waiting for the other shoe to fall.

Brooke thought about the day she had confronted Joe about the blackmail. She had been ready to leave him and figure things out. Had he played her again? Had she fallen for the "poor victim, whose wife had cheated on him" act?

Joe had been so evil for so long, that Brooke now knew she had just been overwhelmed by the whole situation. She wanted a family, but she needed to decide what she was going to do with her life. Frankie had really made her open her eyes. Had Joe really changed?

Her thoughts then turned to Shirley. She was so happy for her. She picked up her phone and pulled up a message from Shirley – it was a screenshot of one of Shirley and Eric's text exchanges, where he told her he had been in love with her all those years ago.

Brooke read the conversation on the screenshot. After everything he had gone through in his life, Eric had told Shirley that she had never left his mind.

She looked up at the top of the shot. Eric's contact information had been caught in the picture. She froze as she realized the number looked familiar. That number was very similar to the hang-up calls and text messages she had received.

She got her phone out and looked in her deleted text messages folder. She had her phone set to not permanently delete them because of possibly losing clients' contact information. There was the text, the one that was sent to her phone when she was with Frankie. The number was the same.

Before she could change her mind, she snuck into Shirley's room and got Shirley's phone. She hoped her friend would forgive her, but Brooke had to know. She went back out on the balcony and clicked in the passcode. It had been the same since the day Reece had been born, his date of birth.

She felt guilty and terrible for doing this. She had discounted Eric from being in her rearview mirror, but had it been him? She opened the text message thread from Eric and Shirley. She read through them.

Eric had known about her and Tom meeting at the park. Her friend had defended her in the responses. Eric had admitted that he hadn't told the police about their encounters. They had talked about the night of the murders. Now Brooke was afraid. She was so confused and didn't know what to think now. Why had Eric contacted her, and what did he want with Shirley? She snuck the phone back into Shirley's room.

The next day, when they got back to town, Brooke dropped Shirley and Reece off at their house. She and Frankie had decided to go see her mom before heading home. Frankie told his grandmother all about the trip. Brooke's mom told him he looked just like his Granddaddy when he told stories.

"I wish Granddaddy was still alive so I could have known him."

Brooke and her mom agreed with Frankie, and they wished the same thing.

Brooke teared up. "They say time heals, and it does, but it's a pain that never goes away."

It was times like this, Brooke wished her dad could see Frankie. She wished her dad was there to help her figure out what to do with her life. They spent over an hour visiting. Her mom loved the sand dollar with a bible verse on it that Frankie had picked out for her from their trip. By the time they left, Brooke and Frankie were ready for a nap.

On the other side of town, Tom's parents were losing hope. Amy's memory was still missing, and the trial would start in a few months. Tom was going to be found guilty at this point, it seemed. Tom's mother admitted that she thought they should look at getting the girls' custody signed over to her and David. She was struggling with the school and getting their updated sports' physicals, with no legal guardianship.

David told her to hold off till the end of summer.

She cried, "My son is going off to prison! We are now raising his teenage girls. How did our life come to this? I hate this so badly for Tom, Amy, and the girls!"

David tried to reassure his wife, even though deep down, he was now thinking time was running out. He promised her he would call the attorney tomorrow. They both prayed for a miracle.

Chapter 24

MEANWHILE, DOWN THE ROAD from the Adcock's house, a man sat at his desk. Tom had been in jail for over three months, and the town would never be able to solve these murders. The Chief really believed that Tom was the true murderer.

The man thought it was the perfect crime.

His first meeting with Ray Harper had been over a year and a half ago. It had been at a bar in Midtown. Ray had apparently drunk more than he realized, and it was very early in the day. The man had only gone there himself to see one of the hot bartenders. She was very easy on the eyes and ears. She kept her mouth shut and he liked that.

Ray had been rambling about someone blowing a five-hundred-million dollar deal.

"This guy is a fucking idiot. How stupid can you be to turn down that kind of offer?"

The man's ears had perked up at the mention of such a large amount of money. He loved money probably more than he loved people. Numbers excited him and something about Ray's rambling made him want to know more.

The man turned and faced Ray and offered to buy him a drink.

"Hey buddy, sounds like you have earned a drink with the kind of day you are having."

Ray laughed and agreed that he had earned much more than a drink.

"I deserve a whole lot more."

Ray started telling the story.

His associate had been offered five-hundred-million dollars for his business, from another company out of Australia, but his associate's partner was unwilling to sell."

Drunkenly, it was hard to follow all of the story, but it had hooked him when he heard "stick it to the idiot" and have control of all the money. The long story short, apparently, Ray and his buddy needed to figure out a way to remove this other partner without paying him a dime.

The man had taken Ray's card and put one of his own in Ray's coat pocket. Possibly this was just some drunk-talking bull but worth finding out. He stood up and told Ray to give him a call if he was serious, anything was possible if you wanted it badly enough.

The man hoped that he would hear back from this guy. Just in case, he would call him if he hadn't heard from him in a few weeks.

Almost two weeks had passed when Ray called. The man smiled - maybe his life would finally have some adventure. The man answered quickly, because he wanted to be a part of this if it involved five-hundred-million dollars. He looked forward to taking advantage of these losers.

Right off the bat, Ray immediately started apologizing for his drunkenness from the day at the bar. Ray barely remembered much, but he remembered hearing that they might have a solution.

"My associate owns part of an extremely successful company." Then Ray told him the rest of the story.

Ray and this associate needed to push out this other partner. The man sat listening and taking notes throughout the hour-long conversation. The call ended with Ray planning to email the partnership contract over as soon as they hung up.

After going through the notes, the man thought that since the company had started years ago, the contract might have some loopholes. This gave him hope. Ray and his associate seemed like deceitful people. He liked that. Although to the man, Ray had just come across as desperate at this point.

Following that call, the man met with Ray and his associate several times over the next several months. Ray had used an alias name and burner phone, also he had never called the man's phone directly after the first call. They wanted to have no connections to each other.

Ray and his associate needed to be extra careful not to have any business dealings with each other, just to be on the safe side.

In the beginning, the man hadn't cared what happened to any of these guys. Greed, and the idea of causing someone mental pain,had excited him.

Throughout the conversations with Ray and his associate, the man was fully aware that this partner would never on his own, break the clause. The others referred to him as a Saint. The man knew firsthand about dealing with people that pretended to be saints. So, it made him want to sink the partner even more.

They needed to figure out how to set him up for embezzlement and get him convicted. Then it would be game over for the other partner. Ray and his associate had even suggested killing him, but the man advised against it – they would get caught.

They all spent months meeting together, while Ray was slowly moving money around. Ray had finally become useful. He was a genius with offshore accounts and setting them up in other people's names. It was also beneficial that the Saint wasn't very cautious about watching the financial part of the business. The Saint trusted the financial accounting team.

Ray just needed to take his time with the money transfers to make it slow enough that it was believable and keep the amount below the "red flag" amount. The offshore account showed three transactions and they were in Tom's name. The dollar amounts mattered because the associate knew the system had alarms set in place to prevent someone from emptying the accounts. Ray's skills were now impressive.

Everything was moving along on target, until the most unbelievable thing happened. Saint Tom started banging his wife.

Chapter 25

JOE LAUGHED OUT LOUD thinking about the irony of the situation. The odds of this situation had to be almost zero percent. Six months prior to the murders, he had hired a private investigator to follow his wife. He didn't trust her at all. You can't trust a person that always does the right thing.

Brooke had to be up to something. He had become suspicious of her, because she was fighting harder against him than she ever had before. Usually, she caved in when he went hard on her because she was too soft. She saw the world through child-like eyes. She deserved his wrath because she needed to grow up.

Last year, Joe had found a loophole in the contract to frame Tom, but it would take some shadiness for it to work. Apparently, the contract was rock solid, and it seemed Tom Adcock had been very cautious.

The contract had a "Termination for Cause" clause. It was very clear that if either partner broke the clause, they would forfeit their part of the business. The contract would give total control to the remaining partner. The clause only listed one ground to execute - a partner must be convicted of a felony for a business-related crime.

Early on, Joe had discovered that Tom lived in Willowville as well, which he thought probably meant he was as big of a hillbilly as his wife. He hated this town and its "coziness", as Brooke called it.

The PI seemed like he wasn't doing his job, as he reported nothing every day for months. But near the end of November, something changed. He had noted some strange activities. Brooke's routine seemed to change. The PI told him he would send the report and some photos later in the day. When the pictures came in, his heart stopped. The picture showed Brooke hugging Saint Tom Adcock.

Now, as he sat, he thought about how he had been a master at making Brooke think he had changed and would be a good husband. She had fallen for all of it. It had been so hard to keep up the charade. He didn't love her, in fact, he didn't even like her. She had been so eager for him to love her that she had eaten it up. She had surprised him when she started to look better. She was even finally trying to look like a woman. That had made it easier to pretend to want her.

Joe had been filled with rage as he thought about the first report on Brooke and Tom's meeting. He wanted to kill them both. He knew he needed to be smart, though. He would not spend his life in prison for either of them. So, he waited for a way to make them pay.

On the morning of the murders, he received a text from Brooke telling him that she would go to the grocery store that evening after she came home to check on Frankie. He knew that meant she would be meeting Tom. Joe knew Brooke was a liar.

Ray and the Parkers were in town for the week, and he was supposed to meet them for dinner. He had convinced them to meet him in Willowville. He had to keep it together, now this was personal. He was about to take Tom down!

Joe was going to make Tom pay. He wanted him to be the one in prison for life.

Tonight was the night. He was lucky in knowing they met every time at the same place – the Private Investigator had sent him detailed reports. So, he texted Ray to finalize the meeting plans.

Joe spent the afternoon planning how he would make sure Tom suffered. He knew from the investigator that the park had no cameras. He had planned the perfect murders. Tom would be the number one suspect if Terry Parker and his wife died.

As soon as Brooke left that night, Joe told Frankie that he would be back. He needed to run to "Grandma's house." Frankie was such a good kid, and he hadn't suspected that Joe was lying.

He drove his truck down to the garage and uncovered the old family car that had belonged to his uncle. Brooke had never even seen the car, since she never came to the garage. The car was black and as plain as they come but was perfect because it had very dark tinted windows.

He loaded up the perfect weapon. His short barrel rifle had a suppressor and a thermal imaging scope. This was one of his favorites. It would be quick, quiet, and had a little longer range, if needed.

Brooke would have freaked out if she had seen Joe's gun collection. She wasn't afraid of guns as she had been raised with a hunter. She would have been afraid of the types of firearms he collected. He even had a target range set up behind the garage.

Joe met Ray and the Parkers at the gas station off the Willowville exit. He arrived a little before they got there and parked in an area that contained no cameras to ensure that no one saw them or their vehicles.

He knew that Ray always got rental cars under fake names so that he couldn't be tracked. Idiots, all of them were idiots.

It was still crowded when they pulled into the park, but he saw Brooke's empty car. His passengers were confused when they parked, but he assured them they needed to see this. He told them they were about to see what Saint Tom was up to, and it would shock them. They all chatted about the embezzlement scheme.

The lot was emptying out now, and the weather was getting worse. It was getting hard to see, but Joe kept his eyes focused.

Once he saw Tom's headlights coming up from a back road, he knew he had to act fast. He got them all out of the car and over to the wood-line area. He knew footprints would never last in this sleet and rain mix. It would also be impossible to track the tire tracks. He silenced them.

"Get ready, you guys are about to be shocked."

Terry recognized Tom's vehicle, and they watched as Brooke climbed out of it. As she was smiling and laughing, even dropping her purse, Joe heard their breathing change. They all knew that wasn't Tom's wife. What they didn't know, though, was that it was Joe's wife. He told them to stay put, he was going to get the car. Brooke never even looked in their direction. He crept back to the car and watched through his imaging scope as Brooke sat in her car.

It was all he could do not to shoot her, but he might need her for a while after this. As Brooke finally pulled out, Joe knew he had to hurry before they all returned to his car. Brooke had made a U-turn, though, which threw him off. Now her car was facing him, so he dropped down out of sight. He peeked up and watched as her taillights showed she was turning onto the main road.

He stuck the gun barrel out the window. The mix of freezing rain and sleet made it nearly impossible to see with the normal eye, but it was easy with his thermal image scope. With one shot, he dropped Ray. Then he immediately aimed at Terry's head and shot.

Two down, he thought. He watched Julie and her chubby-self as she began running towards the gym. He aimed directly at her head, pulled the trigger, and she dropped. He didn't see anyone outside, so he took off immediately.

Now he needed to beat Brooke home and she wasn't the only one that knew these back roads. Earlier in the week, he had found a road that cut off almost fifteen minutes if you drove fast enough. Also, he knew she would be nearly out of gas. He had checked her gauge this morning, and it was very low. He also knew based on the online bank account information, she hadn't bought gas all day with her debit card.

Another thing that helped him beat her home – Brooke drove like an old woman. He made it from the park to his garage with no problem. He parked the car back behind the garage and jumped into his truck. He had just gotten in the front door, when he heard Brooke pulling down the driveway. He raced to the bedroom and laid down on top of the covers.

Tomorrow morning, he would go move the car back into the garage. Brooke never came to bed that night.

By the next day, Joe felt good. Tom's setup was all in process for the embezzlement. With him being at the park, Tom would be the number one suspect for the murders.

Joe had called to fuck with Tom about his family finding out about the affair. He deserved a lot of pain before he moved into his new home in prison. A little blackmail makes people nervous. He wouldn't have to worry about destroying Tom's family, since life would take care of that for him. Tom's pain was worth it all.

The following Sunday after the murders, Brooke was out, and Frankie had been with Shirley. Joe had parked his truck at the gas station, where Ray's rental car was parked. From there, he had driven the rental car back down to the car rental place in the metro area. He had caught a cab back up to his truck.

The town was still not moving much because of the snow. Joe had arrived back home before Brooke got home from the grocery store. She had acted so weird when she returned. Joe had decided he would be on good behavior that night for two reasons: company would be at their house, and he might need Brooke to be on his side if anything went wrong.

It seemed that the plan was working perfectly.

Until he realized he had forgotten one small detail, Larry Jones. The day after Larry had chased Brooke down the back roads, the private investigator had texted Joe that they needed to meet. Joe had immediately remembered that Larry had probably been at the park the night of the murders. He had forgotten because Larry hadn't sent a report that next day. Joe agreed to meet Larry.

This didn't worry him, though. Larry shouldn't have still been following Brooke, and Joe was angry that he had done that. A few days later, Joe handled the problem. He had been grateful to see Larry on his motorcycle. Joe used his car and ran him off the embankment and watched as the motorcycle flamed up. Larry was no longer a threat.

Frankie was the only wild card now. Joe was quite certain that was taken care of too.

Chapter 26

THE WEEK AWAY HAD refreshed her, but Brooke was glad to be home. The beach had been beautiful, and she had enjoyed the trip. She was planning to meet with Shirley for lunch later that day. She needed to find out what Eric was up to. She had decided not to mention it to Shirley, yet.

Brooke hoped there was an explanation for Eric calling her. Shirley deserved to find true love but not with someone who was being shady. She hoped Eric wasn't involved with those killings, but she was going to find out. She also planned on figuring out what was up with Joe and Frankie.

Brooke's thoughts were interrupted, as Joe came out on the porch with her. He had his briefcase in hand.

"I am headed down to the office and to have lunch with my dad."

"Did you miss me?" She asked with a smile.

"What do you mean? It's not like you do anything around here."

She paused and watched his face, "Are you serious?"

"No, I am just playing. I will see you tonight."

Brooke wasn't sure if he was joking, but as she hugged him, she noticed the faint smell of liquor.

When he left, she sat back down on the swing and thought about the night she had returned from the beach. Joe had been strange and distant. Brooke had suspected that he had been drinking then. He had slurred his words and snapped at her. She now knew she had to decide what she would do with her mom, as she would not live with Joe drinking again.

Brooke also didn't want to spend another day not knowing if his actions were real or faked. She wished his words of change could be true, and maybe for him it was. She couldn't live like that anymore. Frankie deserved better.

Brooke was worried about Frankie. His emotional state seemed fragile over the last several months. He had made so many comments about protecting her, and how he would do anything for her. He had talked about how mean his dad was. She wasn't sure, but it seemed like Frankie was hiding something.

Hence, a week away from everything had seemed like heaven. It had also given her a chance to examine her life. Joe had been the same for twenty years, and what if this new attitude was staged.

Now, Brooke was trying to sort everything out. From Joe's change of heart about their marriage, to Frankie's change of heart about his dad and all the other junk surrounding these things.

She thought of Tom, realizing he had been in jail for months now, and she truly didn't believe he was guilty of the things he was charged with. She hoped he would be able to successfully fight the charges.

Brooke headed to the laundry room. It was time to catch up on her chores before meeting Shirley for lunch. There were at least three loads of laundry to do. Frankie would be at camp until late, so she wanted to get as much done as possible.

Brooke shook the sand from the basket. She started a load of clothes and grabbed the broom. The beach always had a way of coming home in your clothes and your car. She began sweeping up the sand and decided to give the whole room a good sweeping.

As she swiped around the dryer, she noticed something sticking out from under the corner of it. When she pulled it out and picked it up, it was a business card holder. The card on top belonged to Larry Jones, Private Investigator, and had his picture on it. She recognized him immediately.

Brooke was dumbfounded and outraged looking at the picture.

This was the man that had followed her, the man she had called Mirror Man. She could see his whole face in her mind now.

When she flipped it over, the card on the other side made her heart stop. She saw Ray Harper's card. He was one of the victims murdered at the park!

Brooke headed straight to her computer and looked up both men. She was shaking. She pulled the cards out of the holder and between them was one of Joe's business cards.

It was then, Brooke realized, when Tom had told her about the blackmail call, she had never asked Joe how he knew about the affair. How could she have been so stupid? Had Joe known the whole time she was meeting with Tom?

The man in the mirror was legally known as Larry Jones, a private investigator. She searched the internet for him and frowned as she read of his unfortunate death. She remembered reading about the motorcycle accident on Hwy 420.

Brooke jumped when she heard the washer buzz. These cards belonged to Joe. She returned to the laundry room and moved the clothes over to the dryer. She turned off her computer and threw on some clean clothes. She didn't want to leave but had to go meet Shirley.

Brooke was more confused than she had ever been. Larry Jones was a private investigator and he had been following her. She thought of the day she almost wrecked when he chased her. She realized the last time she saw him was just a few days before his fatal crash. She wondered whether the accident had been a coincidence.

Brooke brushed her teeth and looked in the mirror. She was caught up in a nightmare. Brooke texted Shirley: **I am on my way.**

Maybe when she got back, she could go down to the garage to see what she could find. How was Joe involved with Ray Harper? She needed to be careful because she had no idea how long Joe would be gone from the house today.

Shirley waved from a table as Brooke entered the restaurant. She was smiling. Brooke was not.

Shirley could tell something was wrong immediately, "What's wrong?"

Brooke sat down and ordered water. She could barely speak.

"It's Joe. It's Eric. It's Tom. It's Frankie. It's LIFE."

"Brooke, honey, what are you talking about?"

Brooke felt ashamed and embarrassed when she admitted that she had gone through Shirley's phone at the beach.

"I don't understand. Why did you go through my phone?"

Shirley was surprised and confused.

"I am sorry! I recognized Eric's number from the screen shot of y'all's text that you had sent me. I wanted to know why he had contacted me and more than once. Then when I read all the things that he had said about me, I needed to know how much he knew."

"Brooke, I get it. We both have serious trust issues with men. I hope you are not going to be mad, but I invited Eric to join us. We can just ask him. He should be here soon."

"Oh!" Brooke said, startled by the news that Eric would be here.

Brooke then told Shirley about Frankie's strangeness the last several months.

"I am worried that Joe is terrorizing him somehow. Frankie had some harsh words about his dad when we were at the beach."

Before they could chat further, Eric walked up to the table. Brooke needed to know why he had called and texted her and what he really knew.

Eric didn't give her a chance to ask. "Hey, Brooke. It's so good to see you." He leaned down and gave Shirley a hug.

"I tried to contact you, but you wouldn't answer." He said to Brooke as he sat down.

"Eric, why did you call me?" Brooke asked him quickly.

"I wanted to talk to you about Shirley. These murders messed with me. I have lost so many people in my life, and I had to take the chance to talk to Shirley."

Shirley smiled and blushed as Eric spoke. Brooke noticed they both looked at each other like love-struck teenagers. Brooke explained how she had been suspicious of Eric, so much so that she had gone through Shirley's phone.

Eric paused before speaking, "You read our texts?"

Brooke nodded.

"I guess you read that I knew about you and Tom. I'm sorry that I spoke out of turn about you guys. Although, I still don't understand how Tom could have cheated on Amy. I have visited with Tom several times since he's been in jail. He feels terrible for hurting everyone, like he has. I am working with his attorney to be a character witness."

"I hope he can figure out a way to win his case. I hate this for everyone. I found something that may help Tom. I was sweeping my laundry room this morning, and I found some business cards."

"I don't think any business cards are gonna help Tom!" Eric said with a confused look on his face.

"One of the cards belonged to RAY HARPER! One of the victims from the park!"

"Holy shit! Why would Ray's card be in your laundry room?" Eric questioned.

"Exactly! I don't know, but I intend to find out. Also, there was another card, it belonged to the man from my rearview mirror."

"The man that chased you? What has he got to do with this?" Shirley said as she shook her head. This was bonkers to her!

"I think he may have been at the park, following me, for Joe! My mind has just been warped since that night. He was a private investigator, and I think Joe hired him."

"Holy shit! That asshole has probably known about the affair for a while! I can't believe he didn't blow up on you! Why do you think he didn't immediately come after you?" Shirley snapped.

"I don't know, but I intend to find out!"

They all realized they were being too loud, and people were starting to look.

"I have a plan. Joe is working at his law firm office. I called his dad on my way here, acting like I was checking on them, and they had just gotten back to the office from lunch with a new client. That should at least buy me another hour or so. When I get home, I am going to go down to his garage. I have to pick up Frankie, so I can't stay long. I should be okay."

"Brooke! What if that bastard catches you down there?" Shirley was terrified.

"I should be okay. I am going to walk down there and leave my car in the drive, so if Joe comes home early, he will hopefully go to the house first. I promise I will text you if anything goes wrong. Otherwise, I will text you on my way to get Frankie."

Shirley hugged her as they stood in the restaurant parking lot.

"Please be careful. I love you."

"I have to do this, you know that. For everyone involved, I have to find out how Joe is connected. I love you! Just promise me that no matter what, if something happens to me, you will get Frankie and run if you have to."

Brooke left the restaurant determined to find out how Joe was involved and hopefully, to find evidence to clear Tom.

She went in and changed into her tennis shoes instead of the flip-flops she had worn to lunch. Frankie would be done with camp in less than three hours. She hoped that Joe would see her car at the house and head there first.

Brooke jogged through the woods down to Joe's garage. She hadn't seen it in years. She snuck up through the back side. She noticed that Joe had a target range set up behind the building.

My God, she thought, how weird since he had always been so against guns in their house. She had no idea that Joe even owned a gun. He had not allowed a gun in their home since they had first been married. She thought they needed one for protection, but he had refused.

The garage was massive. She didn't remember it being so big, when it was first built. Brooke snuck around to the front door. She knew where the key was hidden – Joe was very predictable. She unlocked the door and eased in. She went to get her phone to check the time and realized she had left it at home. She cursed herself, she felt foolish.

She had never cared to go in the garage before, but was blown away when she walked in. She thought it would be your typical man's cave, but it was not. The first thing she noticed was the distinct smell. It was clean but had a distant smell of cigars that hung in the air.

To the right of her was a small bar and behind it was a mirror that covered the whole wall with shelves full of liquor. On the other side of her was a sitting area full of massive furniture and faux brick covering the wall. Art covered much of the brick. It was beautiful and very masculine.

She walked beyond the large room into a hallway, on each side were two doors. She tried to go into the first doors, to the right and left, but they were both locked. She was surprised when the third door opened. Behind the door looked like Joe's office. All four of the walls in this room were covered with large pin-up girl prints. The frames on the prints appeared expensive, as did everything in this garage.

Brooke sat down at the desk and started looking through the files. Her eyes grew wide when she noticed one of the folders was labeled "Saint Tom". She tried to swallow but her mouth was dry.

She opened the file and started reading. Each page caused her more rage. There on the pages was a step by step process of how he and these men had set up Tom for embezzlement. Oh my God, Brooke thought. The words were popping off the page as she read. Terry, Tom's partner, was part of the scheme. He was one of the other victims, as well as Ray Harper! Brooke couldn't process all of the information included in the file. She gasped when she got to the pages where Joe had detailed out killing the Parkers and Ray Harper. He had planned all of this, and he was setting Tom up for murder and embezzlement.

Joe was a murderer. Tom was innocent. She panicked and was too afraid to remove anything from the desk. She closed the folder and stuck it back, where she had found it. She cursed herself again for forgetting her phone.

She felt sick as she continued to search. She then found a large box on a shelf behind the desk. When she opened the box, it contained some type of fancy automatic rifle with a scope and what she thought might be a silencer. She wanted to vomit.

Brooke was about to scream, but before she could, she heard Joe's truck. The mufflers were so loud, and for the first time since he bought the truck, she was grateful for the warning.

She could barely breath - fear filled her lungs. She had to hurry, as she didn't have much time. There was a side window off to the back of the office. She ran to the window and pushed it open. She climbed out and the drop was more than she expected it to be. The fall nearly broke her arm as she hit the ground and landed on something sharp.

She looked down and saw blood pouring from her arm. She crawled over to a tarp that was lying on the ground. She got under it as fast as she could. She prayed that she hadn't left a trail of blood. The truck had turned off. She then realized that she hadn't locked the front door back.

Joe's voice was now echoing in the air, "Hello? Is someone out here?"

He must have noticed the door was unlocked. She held her breath as she heard his footsteps on some leaves still left on the ground. He had continued to walk, and was standing right next to the tarp. He took a few more steps and was now standing on the tarp. He paused. Brooke's pulse was racing, and her arm was throbbing. She could hear Joe breathing, he was so close. She worried that he could hear her heart, it was pounding so hard.

Then she saw his foot pressed only inches away from her. She couldn't move without being caught. After what seemed like an eternity, he turned and started walking back in the other direction. She didn't know how long she had lay there, but she knew she needed to get home so that she could go get Frankie.

She eased herself to where she could look out. There was no sign of Joe. She could see a corner of his truck. She needed to get out of here. Joe was a killer! She knew he wouldn't mind killing her. She crawled on her stomach trying to not make a sound as she made her way to the wooded area. As soon as she was far enough away from the garage, she ran with everything she had.

While still running back home, she heard the truck crank. When she heard the truck, she tried to look over her shoulder to the driveway area, and tripped over a log. She hit the ground hard. Her body was aching. She willed herself to get up and go. She managed to stand up and continued to run.

She was panting by the time she entered through the back door. She knew that Joe would be there any minute. When she entered the house, she was relieved to see she still had time to go get Frankie. She grabbed a long sleeve shirt from the laundry room to cover her arm. She continued through the house to grab her purse and her phone as she headed straight out the front door.

She could hear Joe calling her from his truck parked behind the house. She kept walking down the driveway towards her car.

"Brooke!" He yelled.

She was scared he would see all the blood and see how hard she was sweating. She yelled over her shoulder, "Hey, I can't talk. I've got to hurry to get Frankie from camp."

He continued to watch her, as she could feel his eyes still on her. She cranked her car and backed out as quickly possible. When she reached the end of the driveway, she put the car in park. She let out a scream and the tears poured.

As she cried, she found a towel from Frankie's bag in the car, and wrapped her arm. God help her and Frankie, they were in a lot of danger. And now, did Joe suspect she had been at the garage? Had she left blood on the window or the tarp?

She dialed Shirley. They needed to meet as soon as they picked up the boys. Shirley suggested they go to Brooke's mom's house so that the boys could play.

Brooke looked like a mess. Her hair was drenched with sweat.

Frankie noticed the blood and how disheveled his mom looked, when he climbed in her car.

"Mom, are you okay?"

She nodded. "I'm okay, sweetheart. I just fell before I came to get you."

Frankie didn't seem like he believed her.

"You look like you were in a car wreck! Did Dad do this to you?"

"Why would you think your Dad would hurt me?"

Brooke stopped and watched as her son's body tensed.

"Frankie, I want to ask you something. Do you have any secrets that I don't know about?"

He shook his head no, but shrugged. "I don't want to talk about it, Mom."

They sat silently for what seemed like forever.

"Frankie, I have some secrets that you don't know about."

He looked at her hard as she spoke.

"You mean what you did with the killer guy?"

She laughed, "No not that one, everyone knows about that. I mean about your Dad."

His body jerked at her words.

"I don't understand why you are so mad at your dad. Has he ever asked you to do something, that made you uncomfortable?"

Tears started to roll from his eyes. "I am scared to tell you my secrets about Dad. I don't want you to go away forever."

Now she knew, Joe was blackmailing their son as well.

"Frankie, I need to know your secrets, and one day I will share all of mine with you."

Frankie told his story for the remainder of the drive to Brooke's mom's house. Joe had left the night of the murders, right after she had left to go meet Tom. Joe had threatened Frankie that if he ever told anyone, then his mom would disappear forever. Brooke was devastated as she heard his story. She assured Frankie that she wasn't going anywhere, and that everything was going to be okay. No matter what she had to do, they were going to get through this.

"I need you to trust me. I love you!" Brooke added.

Frankie nodded. "I believe you, Mom."

Chapter 27

Brooke and Shirley sat on her mom's porch. The boys were out in the front yard building a fort. Shirley was shocked when she saw Brooke.

Brooke hadn't said a word since Shirley arrived. Shirley waited patiently as she knew it was bad. They had gone in and doctored Brooke's arm. It looked like it might need stitches, but Brooke had just kept bandaging it. She changed into some clothes she had borrowed from her mom.

Brooke finally spoke, "Joe is a murderer!"

Shirley almost shouted, "What the fuck! What do you mean? I don't understand!"

Brooke told her about the afternoon. She cried as she told her about climbing out the window and hurting her arm, she had been terrified. She also remembered that she had left the window open as well as the front door open. Joe would know someone had been in there.

They spent the next hour trying to make a plan. It seemed impossible, but everything had a solution. Brooke's mom had joined them, and they filled her in on everything. Her mom was afraid of her going back to her house, but Brooke told her she had to for now. She took a gun from her father's collection - a small handgun. It would only work in a very short range situation. She planned on keeping it in her pocket.

Frankie was going to go home with Shirley, so that he would be safe. Brooke stayed late at her mom's house so that Joe was asleep when she got home.

The next day, Brooke stayed outside, working on her flowerbeds until after Joe left. Shortly after, Shirley came over to help. The plan was if Shirley heard Joe drive up, she had to text Brooke.

Brooke headed to the garage again. This time the hidden key had been moved but was still easy enough to find.

When she went in the garage, though, everything in the office was gone. The gun box and the papers had been removed. She needed to talk to the Chief, but would he believe her? He would probably think she was trying to protect Tom.

Her phone pinged. Frankie had texted: **MOM, Dad just called me to see how I was. Well, he really was just making sure I remembered to keep our secret or else. He said he was on his way home.** Brooke was surprised Joe had called Frankie, although she was grateful for the warning.

It made her angry thinking about how Joe had been treating Frankie.

She quickly headed out and this time made sure it was locked, as well as the key put back exactly where it had been. She was running through the woods and back to the house. Hatred filled her. She finally thought of an idea, but she didn't know if it would work.

Brooke headed straight into the house, "Joe just called Frankie and he is headed home, right now. I don't know how long we have!"

"Oh, shit! Let's just say that you are sick, and I came over to help you," Shirley suggested.

"I knew that Joe must have suspected something, because all of the evidence from before when I was there is gone." Brooke said as she threw her housecoat on and put blush on her cheeks to appear feverish. She was still sweaty from the hike to and from his garage.

Shortly after, both women were pacing the room when they heard Joe's truck pull in.

"You got this, just remember how much is at stake and keep that gun on you, no matter what."

The back door opened, and Joe walked in. He looked from Brooke, who was now laying on the couch, to Shirley.

"What's going on?" He asked slowly, "Is everything okay?"

Joe was now staring at Brooke, noticing her red face and how sweaty she appeared.

Brooke put her hand in her pocket. The cold metal from the gun made her more aware of how dangerous this all was.

"Hey, I was about to text you. I started running a fever and throwing up after you left this morning."

Brooke could feel her legs shaking, she couldn't imagine how in the hell she was going to get through this.

"I called Shirley, and she came over with some nausea medication that she had. I took it and now just praying this passes quickly."

"Sick? You seemed fine this morning?" Joe barked.

"Joe, she's been throwing up! You know how quickly viruses can come on." Shirley added.

Shirley was starting to panic. Joe didn't seem empathetic, and she wasn't sure he was buying their story.

"It still doesn't make sense to me, that you could get so sick this quickly."

Brooke stood up, afraid this was about to turn ugly.

"Joe..."

"I don't really give a damn either way, I am going down to my garage." Joe started towards the back door. He stopped and turned around.

"Oh, by the way, were you down at my garage?" Joe studied her as he asked.

Brooke's phone rang and she grabbed it to keep from answering Joe. It was her mom.

She heard the back door close, told her mom she would call later, hung up, and collapsed against Shirley.

Over the next few days, Brooke continued to fake sickness, but didn't know how much more she could take. She was ready to kill Joe, herself. She had never been this scared or mad about anything.

The next day, Joe was working at his downtown office. He had a bottle full of alcohol in his hand. He thought about the past few days. He still wondered if Brooke had been in his garage. He was sure that he had locked the door on his last visit. He also raised the windows sometimes to let in some fresh air, but it was unusual that he forgot and left it fully open. He had drank a lot the day before, maybe he had just forgotten to close it.

He had made sure to lock everything up since then, and made sure no evidence was lying around. The other odd thing was that Brooke had been acting very strange these last few days. She claimed to be sick, and she had been sleeping in the guest room.

He had tried to go in there to her the night before, but she had locked the door. This morning, he had asked her about it, but she claimed that she didn't know it was locked. Then when he tried to hug her, she pushed him away, claiming she didn't want to make him sick with whatever she had.

Now sitting at his desk, he was ready to get the hell away from this redneck family and town. He knew that would have to wait. Everything was under control. Tom was still sitting in jail, and that made him happy. He would walk away from all of them soon, but he wanted to stay until after Tom's trial.

The mail for the day was stacked up at the front office, and he went to grab it on his way out the door. One of the pieces was a large manila envelope addressed to him. He noticed his father had the same one in his stack. He assumed it was someone selling something.

On his way home, Joe stopped at the liquor store. They all knew him well. Thinking about it, they treated him more like family than his own did. He chatted with the owner. Joe was a regular there, and everyone always enjoyed talking with him.

Back home, down in his garage, Joe started thinking about how it all was working perfectly. His emotions were rising with each sip he took. He had succeeded with his plan. Tom would be convicted soon of embezzlement and then murder. Then Joe would be free and could go on a new adventure. He smiled as he thought, maybe he could take the hot bartender with him.

As he started rifting through his mail, his eyes caught the large envelope again. It was not from a marketer. It was handwritten with a marker. He opened the envelope slowly. The envelope contained a folded letter inside. He unfolded the letter, and read the note.

Greetings Mr. Bradley, Willowville Chief of Police, Brooke, and Joe:

Most of you do not know me. My name is Larry Jones. I am a private investigator primarily working out of the metropolitan zip code.

I was hired by Joe Bradley. My job seemed simple – follow his wife, Brooke, to find out if she was having an affair. When she spotted me on the night of the murders, she did not have any idea who I was.

I continued to follow her a few more times as I wanted to warn her about her husband. Unfortunately, if you are reading this, it means that I am no longer here on this earth.

I gave specific instructions for this to be mailed on this day if I was no longer here. I can only hope I went peacefully, although I nervously knew Joe might take care of me.

I witnessed Joe shoot all three victims the night at Mining Mill Park. I hope justice is served. The pictures to prove it are on their way.

Joe, I hope you pay dearly for all of the pain you have caused.

Sincerely, Larry Jones

The letter was short but to the point. It had been sent to him, his father, Brooke, and the Chief. Now they all knew. Joe knew his father would not show him any mercy for this.

Rage filled Joe! How had he not thought of Larry on the night of the murders? He had been so sure that he had taken care of Larry! No one would have ever tracked any of this to him before this letter.

Tom Adcock was going to get away with fucking his wife.

"Fuck you all!" He screamed as sweat rolled down his face.

Joe reached into his desk top drawer. He pulled out his small handgun. He would not give his father or Brooke the satisfaction of seeing him go down. Sitting back, he put the gun into his mouth and pulled the trigger.

Chapter 28

THE MORNING FOLLOWING THE police raid of Joe's garage, the Chief sat at his desk. He looked at the large envelope still sealed in a stack of mail on his desk. He had read a copy of the letter that Brooke had given him yesterday morning when he arrived at the scene.

The previous morning, his phone had rang very early. It had been Brooke. During the call, she was screaming and he could hardly understand a word she said. He had told her to calm down and he had headed straight to her house. The Chief had called in for back-up, not knowing what they were walking into.

The scene was gruesome. Joe had apparently taken the gun in his mouth. A bloody copy of the letter had also been lying on Joe's desk. The Chief shook his head, thinking about the scene he had found in the garage. It was horrific. He felt horrible for Brooke, as she had vomited several times throughout the morning.

He gave her time to gather herself, before taking her statement.

She tried to explain to him how it had all come about. Brooke stated that she had gotten the letter in the mail and had read it the night before - she had been confused by it.

After reading the letter, she had googled Larry Jones and found out that he was the man that she had seen the night at the park and the other times after that. She also saw he was deceased. It seemed he had crashed in Willowville on his motorcycle, just months ago. She tried to call Joe multiple times last night, but he never answered.

The next morning, when Joe hadn't come home, she had decided to go down to the garage to check on him. His truck was there, but the garage was quiet. She went to the door and knocked, because Joe would have been angry with her if she hadn't. She had broken down more before she continued speaking. When she finally turned the knob, the door had opened as it was not locked. She searched around until she found the door that led into his office. It was shut but not locked, Brooke had opened the door and had almost collapsed.

Joe's garage became a crime scene. The whole building and its perimeter had been yellow-taped off. Most of the rooms were locked, and had to be busted into. The area around Joe's body was a bloody mess.

The garage contained enough evidence to close the murder case against Tom. In one of the locked rooms, Joe had left files surrounding the embezzlement scheme and notes on how to set Tom up with murder. The murder weapon was in a box in the same room.

The Chief hadn't trusted his gut, he never believed Tom was guilty, and had arrested an innocent man. No weapon would have ever been found, had it not been for the letter from Larry Jones.

Tom was being released this morning. The Chief had spoken to the district attorney and to Tom's attorney. He was so thankful this nightmare was over, for Tom and his family. He had called Steve, out in Texas, to advise them of the situation, as well.

The Chief also knew Brooke had a ways to go before her nightmare ended. The Chief thought about the day Joe had come in with Brooke. He had seemed so calm and had given no signs of anything other than that of a supportive husband. Another reminder that he had missed a clue.

Brooke's son, Frankie, had talked with the Chief and let him know that he knew his dad had left that night, but had been pressed to keep it a secret. Apparently, Joe had been tormenting Frankie about never saying a word about Joe leaving that night of the murders. Frankie and Brooke were going to need a lot of support to get through all of this, the Chief thought. He had no doubt, this community would help them.

The Chief picked up his cell phone and dialed David's number.

"David, it's the Chief. I have some awesome news and I wanted to tell you myself. I am sorry for everything that has happened. Tom should be released within the next hour or so."

"OH MY GOD, are you serious?" My son is free!" David exclaimed.

The Chief told David the whole story and then they discussed the paperwork that had to be completed before Tom's release.

The Chief was trying to wrap his head around all of this. This private investigator had solved a case that would have probably convicted an innocent man solely on circumstantial evidence. He shook his head. Guilt filled him over his failure.

He was relieved that this was now over. The Chief had decided over the last twenty-four hours to retire at his thirtieth anniversary in November. He had served this community as best as he had known how.

This case had taught him that things aren't always as they seem. Everyone seemed to have learned the dangers of being somewhere that you weren't supposed to be.

The Chief stood and went down to the office where Tom would be released. When Tom entered, he apologized that it had taken this long to get him released. The Chief hugged Tom.

The Chief said to him, "I'm so sorry you got caught up in this horrible scandal. I hate that someone caused our town to divide. I pray you, Amy, and the girls can move past this. My wife and I will continue to pray for Amy's health."

Tom was grateful, as he told the Chief, "I am just relieved that this is over!"

Tom met his father in the lobby, and they walked to the car. David held his son for what seemed like forever before they headed to meet his girls at David's house.

When they pulled into the driveway, the girls met Tom at the car. Both fell into him, as they all cried.

"My son! I can't believe it's over!! Praise God, it's over." Sylvia hugged him. She now stood watching them and thanking God. They had gotten the miracle they prayed for.

"Would you guys be mad, if I go on over to the hospital? I need to see Amy!"

Everyone agreed that they understood. The girls wanted to go home. He said he would drop them on the way to the hospital. His parents watched as they drove off.

Chapter 29

WHEN THEY ARRIVED HOME, Tom and the girls went inside. They all shouted with joy at being home. Tom decided to take a shower, and dress before going to the hospital. He wondered if he would ever stop crying. Tears rolled as he showered.

He thought about the Parkers. Terry had been framing him all along. He had seen copies of the evidence from Joe's desk.

Tom still didn't understand the details behind it but was grateful his business was safe. He thought about how ironic it was that Brooke's husband, Joe, had been involved in trying to frame him months before the affair with Brooke even started.

When Tom got to the hospital, Amy lit up as she saw him walk in. He grabbed her and lifted her from the floor. She cried happy tears.

"Tom, I thought you were dead, and they just weren't telling me!"

Amy's arms remained wrapped around him.

"I am so sorry I haven't been able to visit!"

She wanted him to tell her what was going on. He told her they needed to talk to her doctor first before they could discuss anything. For now, he just wanted to hold her.

Luckily, they didn't have to wait long. Dr. Tyler was making his rounds and stuck his head in the door. He was happy to see a smile on Amy's face that he hadn't seen before.

Tom and the doctor stepped into the hallway. They walked as they talked about Amy.

Dr. Tyler said, "Amy is ready to go home - I would think by the end of the week. I want to make sure her bloodwork is good. The anti-depressants that she is taking could cause some serious side effects."

Tom nodded as he listened, although he felt lost, not understanding her medical condition.

"Amy was a mess when she arrived. Given the circumstances, it was understandable. I am so glad for your family that the charges against you have been dropped. I think we need to let the counselor guide the conversation with Amy to let her know what's been going on during her memory loss."

"Whatever we need to do. I just want my wife to get better."

When he came back into her room, Amy curled up to him. He told her it wouldn't be long before they were all home.

She asked him, "Is our marriage, okay?"

He pulled her close, and replied in her ear, "Better than ever."

She smiled and fell asleep next to him.

That night, Amy woke up startled and had dreamed of Tom. The nurse was in the room and let her know Tom was fine.

"He will be back in the morning to go to counseling with you."

Amy knew whatever memories she was missing must be bad. She dreamed of the snow often and sometimes of Tom's partner, Terry, and his wife. She didn't know why she dreamed of them so often, but the thought of Terry's wife, Julie, gave her anxiety and she didn't know why.

The thoughts were making her pulse race now. She tried to go back to sleep. Tom would be here in less than three hours. He would fix everything. She loved him so much. Just seeing him had instantly calmed her - it had given her more peace than she had felt in so long.

When Tom arrived, Amy was looking out the hospital room window.

She turned, "I have to know everything today, Tom. I can't live like this anymore. The missing memories are keeping me from healing."

She spoke softly, and Tom agreed.

Sitting with the counselor was painful. Tom admitted to Amy, he hadn't visited her because he had been in jail because he had been accused of murder.

Amy had cried and suddenly froze as she remembered and yelled out.

"Oh my God, Tom, you killed three people, embezzled money from your company, and had an affair!"

Tom stopped her.

"Honey, I didn't kill anyone, and I didn't steal any money from anyone. All the charges have been dropped."

Amy surprised him when she spoke, "But how were the charges dropped? You did it."

The counselor was just as surprised. Amy was getting physically upset. She remembered all of it. Julie Parker had been blackmailing and terrorizing her. The memories were flooding back.

"Amy, I didn't kill anyone."

Amy looked at him. "I know you were there that night. Please don't lie to me anymore. I was there, Tom. I saw you leave with Brooke and then I headed home. You were gone for a long time."

Tom frowned as Amy Spoke.

Amy continued, "Julie had texted me last year before your computer broke. She had texted that we needed to talk. She told me you and Terry were doing something shady with the company. She also told me that y'all were hiding money and planning on leaving us."

"She called me every day after that talk. She made it all sound so true. She called one day and said she had figured out a way to fix it. She had me go into your office while you were out with the girls. I went on your computer, and Julie walked me through each step to put a virus on your computer."

"It apparently worked as you got a new computer three days later. You gave me the boxed computer to send back to the office, but Julie had me label it to her home address."

"Then I got nervous, and I didn't believe you would betray me, so I told Julie, I was done working with her. She was furious. She told me that I had committed a crime and P & A Tech could press charges against me. That went on for months, and then she started threatening to hurt me and the girls."

"Harm you and the girls? I wish I would have known!" Tom interrupted.

"I was finally ready to confess to you and face the consequences, but Julie started sending me texts proving she knew my exact location. She was watching me. She told me I would be killed if I said a word to you. I even began studying crime pods to find a solution."

Amy paused, her head dropped. "Then you started to meet Brooke. I thought you had lied about all of it. When you told me everything about the embezzlement charges, the murders, and the affair, it lined up with Julie's story. I thought you had

235

fooled me. I was going crazy. I even bought a gun! I was so scared of all of you by then."

Amy stopped talking – tears were flowing. The counselor suggested a break. She left the room.

"Amy, I am so sorry for all of this! I cheated on you, but Brooke's husband, Joe, killed all three of them and they all had set me up for embezzlement."

She looked confused at him, "Brooke's husband? That doesn't make any sense!"

Tom told her he had only been at the park meeting Brooke. She admitted she had seen him there, because she had followed him.

They spent the next hour putting everything together. Now he knew how they had his computer. It broke his heart, and made him angry at the damage they had caused his family.

The counselor agreed to go to Dr. Tyler, so he could get Amy released today. She thought the best thing for her would be to go home with Tom and her girls.

Chapter 30

ONE YEAR LATER, ON the anniversary of the murders, Brooke was sitting on her porch. It was much warmer tonight than it had been on that dreadful night. It was almost sixty degrees as the sun was starting to set.

One more reminder that you never knew what to expect with the weather in Georgia. She sat with her coffee cup in hand.

Frankie had gone to Shirley's house after basketball practice to spend the night. Brooke had spent the afternoon visiting her mom.

Her mom was doing amazingly well. The new medicine had really made a difference. She only needed a cane now, as she no longer used a wheelchair. She was able to go out on short trips and had been coming over to Brooke's house once a week for dinner.

Brooke looked over at the wheelchair ramp built after Joe's death. It was built the week of Joe's funeral. Her mom had wanted to come be with her and Frankie. Brooke's mom knew Joe had changed and had treated Brooke horribly after her father died. But Brooke hadn't told her how bad things were or why she was putting up with it.

After Joe's death, Brooke told her mom everything. Her mother had felt enormously guilty, for all these years of abuse Brooke had suffered due to her health problems. She had been grateful to her son-n-law and daughter at the time, but at what cost to Brooke. Brooke had assured her it was ok – she loved her and would have done anything to help her.

Brooke's life changed forever, when she ran into Tom at the rally. He had given her confidence and made her want more out of her life. It had given her the desire to live her life. She had no idea then how much it was going to change.

Tom and Amy were still together. Brooke was happy for Tom. They deserved happiness. She had seen them around town some and both appeared smitten.

Some guilt still haunted her that she had allowed herself to have an affair. Sometimes you just make stupid mistakes. Being with Tom had been a mistake. They both had paid dearly for being where they shouldn't have been.

Brooke thought about Joe. His funeral had been small. She had cried from grief and relief. Frankie had cried and felt responsible in some way. They had gone to therapy together since then, and it helped them both process all that had happened. They just took it one day at a time.

Joe's parents had been very ashamed of all that had gone down. It had made national news as two of the victims were from Texas. Joe's dad had approached Brooke during the week of Joe's funeral activities – he had handed her a check. The amount was large and appreciated but no amount could make up for the things Joe had done.

He told Brooke how sorry they were, and they wanted to make it up to Frankie. They loved Brooke and their grandson. Joe had always been a difficult child. She heard his mother say, house devil and street angel. Hearing her say that was strange since Brooke had thought that for years.

Luckily, Joe had set up some accounts that were in her name, to hide money. He had probably used funds from his family's business illegally, but Mr. Bradley had not wanted to investigate. They wanted her and Frankie to be able to live a good life.

She now had enough money to put away for their future. She had gone back to work a few weeks after Joe's funeral. She was doing well at work, and staying busy kept her mind from reliving everything.

She thought about Larry Jones, the man in the mirror, and she frowned at his unfortunate death. She believed it was not an accident, but the Chief was not able to find any full proof to prove it. She was positive that Larry had been killed by Joe. It didn't matter now, as Joe was gone forever.

Larry Jones had ultimately been her lifesaver. Brooke had pulled the trigger in Joe's death.

No, she hadn't pulled the trigger that killed Joe, but she had written those letters from Larry and had mailed them.

Since she didn't know what Larry had seen the night at the park, she had kept the letters short. She mailed one to the Chief, one to Joe's Dad, one to herself, and one to Joe.

She had hoped it would cause the police to investigate Joe, and hopefully they could find something to connect Joe to the murders. She hadn't known the avalanche of events that her bluff would cause. When she got home that day and saw the envelope to herself, she knew that everyone else would have gotten theirs. She called Joe several times, but there was no answer.

She waited until the next morning, when Joe hadn't come home that night, and drove down to his garage. Expecting that he was passed out from drinking, she couldn't believe it when she opened the door, and vomited at the sight of Joe.

There was blood everywhere. Joe was dead. He had shot himself. She hadn't known how sick in the head he had been. She had sobbed for a while, before finally, dialing the Chief. He told her to stay calm and not to touch anything.

From there, everything became a circus around her. The cops and the ambulance showed up. Joe's garage became a crime scene. Busting all the locked areas, they found a large collection of military style rifles, paperwork, and enough evidence to know Joe was guilty of the murders and the embezzlement setup.

Joe had almost gotten away with the perfect crime. She felt a sudden flare of happiness now, thinking how no one ever questioned the letters or the pictures that never followed. The Chief may have known they were not legitimate, but he never said a word with all the other proof they had. The letter no longer mattered.

Brooke and Frankie both promised that they would never have secrets from each other. Brooke knew it was a lot for a boy his age, but he deserved to know the whole truth. She would always be grateful that she had the only good thing that had ever come from Joe, her son Frankie.

She smiled up to Heaven. Her daddy would have been proud of her bravery. She was in control of her life now. She had survived a nightmare, but she was finally free.

Made in the USA
Columbia, SC
09 April 2024